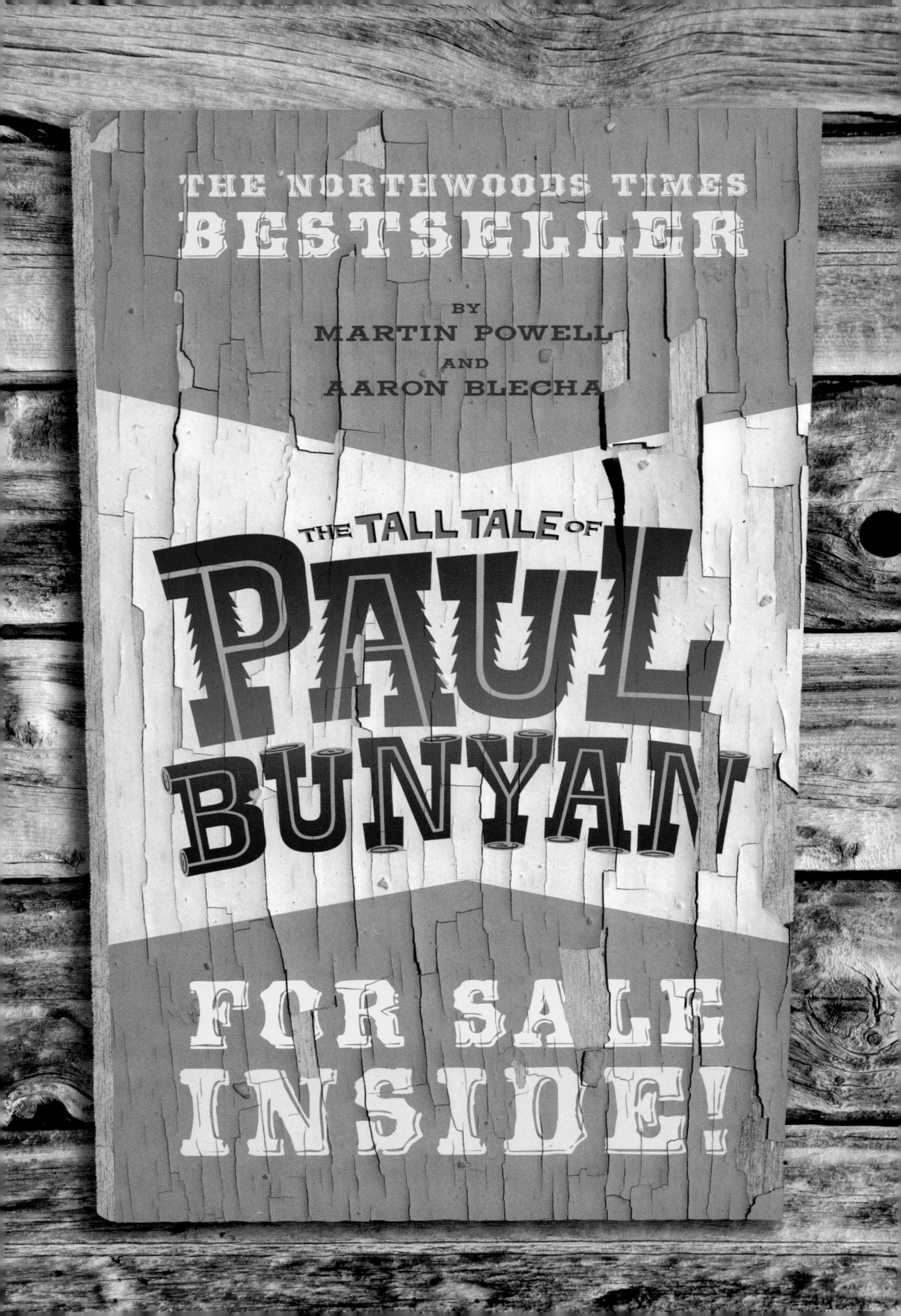
THE NORTHWOODS TIMES
BESTSELLER
BY
MARTIN POWELL
AND
AARON BLECHA
THE TALL TALE OF
PAUL
BUNYAN
FOR SALE
INSIDE!

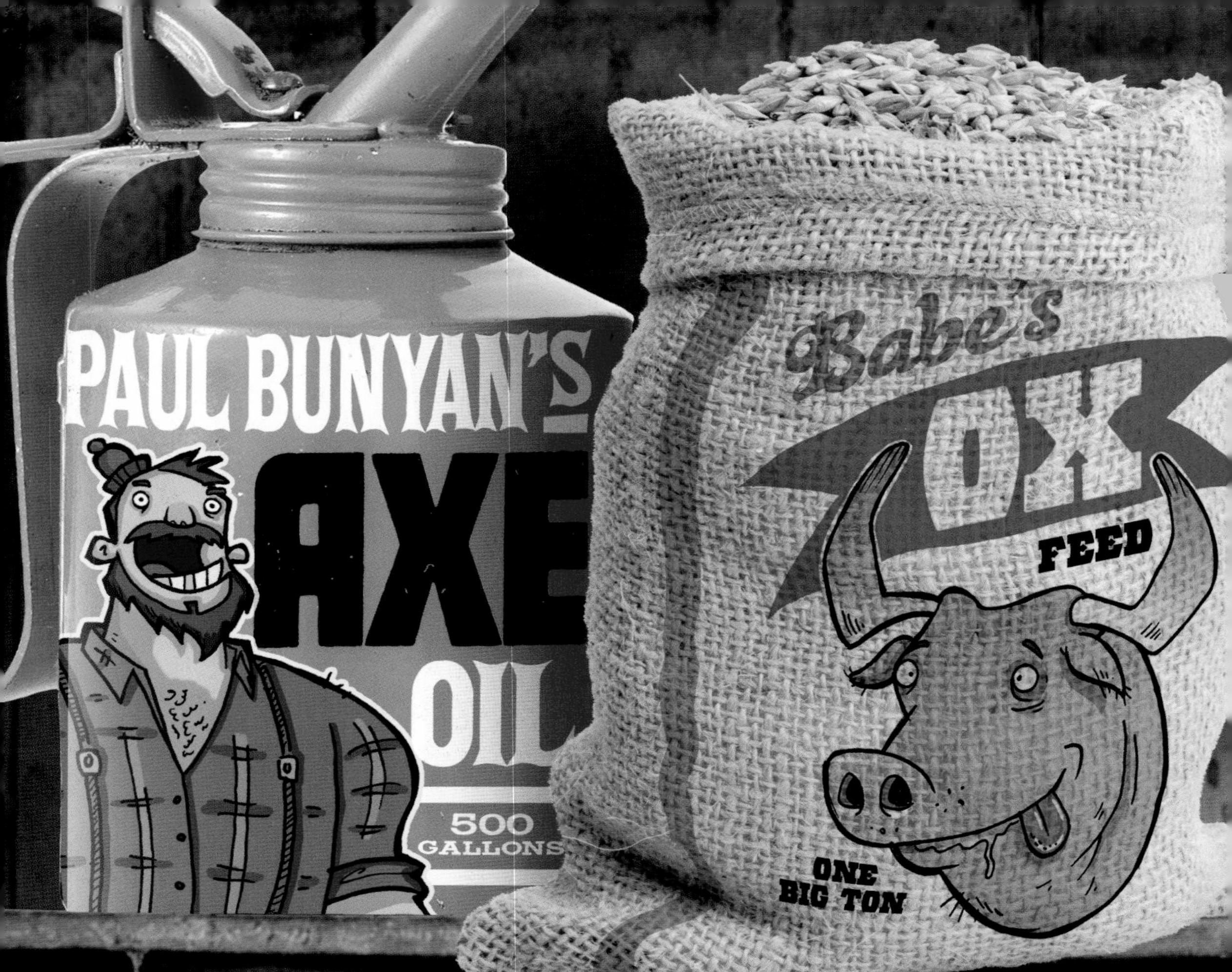
PAUL BUNYAN'S
AXE
OIL
500
GALLONS
Babe's
OX
FEED
ONE
BIG TON

Graphic Spin
is published by Stone Arch Books – A Capstone Imprint
151 Good Counsel Drive, P.O. Box 669
Mankato, Minnesota 56002
www.capstonepub.com

Library of Congress Cataloging-in-Publication Data
Powell, Martin.
The tall tales of Paul Bunyan : the graphic novel / retold by Martin Powell ; illustrated by Aaron Blecha.
p. cm. -- (Graphic spin)
ISBN 978-1-4342-1897-1 (library binding) -- ISBN 978-1-4342-2268-8 (pbk.)
1. Bunyan, Paul (Legendary character)--Legends. 2. Graphic novels. [1. Graphic novels. 2. Bunyan, Paul (Legendary character)--Legends. 3. Folklore--United States. 4. Tall tales.] I. Blecha, Aaron, ill. II. Title.
PZ7.7.P69Tal 2010
741.5'973--dc22 2009029329

Printed in the United States of America in Stevens Point, Wisconsin.
102010 005977R

Summary: The legendary woodsman Paul Bunyan was the biggest man who ever lived. He had wagon wheels for shirt buttons, and his axe took an entire town a whole year to build! One day, Paul finds a big blue ox frozen in the snow. He nurses the behemoth back to health, and names his new companion Babe. The two travel the land, and clear the way for settlers who will soon follow.

Photo Credits: Shutterstock/aaaah, AKaiser, balaikin, bodgdan ionescu, Brett Mulcahy, Bruce Amos, c., charles taylor, Clint Cearley, Dmitrijs Mihejevs, freelanceartist, frescomovie, jadimages, Kalim, Lagui, marekuliasz, Nanka (Kucherenko Olena), Olivier Le Queinec, Ronald Sumners, Sebastian Crocker, TeplouhovJurij, Vladimir Wrangel

Designer & Art Director: Bob Lentz
Creative Director: Heather Kindseth
Editor: Donald Lemke
Production Specialist: Michelle Biedscheid

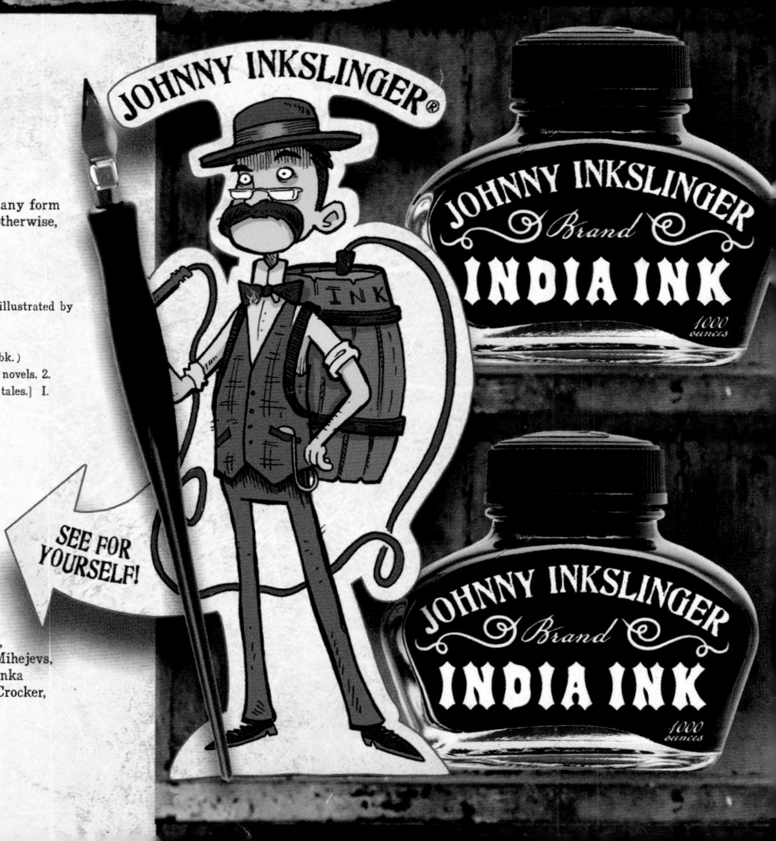
JOHNNY INKSLINGER®
INK
SEE FOR YOURSELF!
JOHNNY INKSLINGER
Brand
INDIA INK
1000 ounces
JOHNNY INKSLINGER
Brand
INDIA INK
1000 ounces

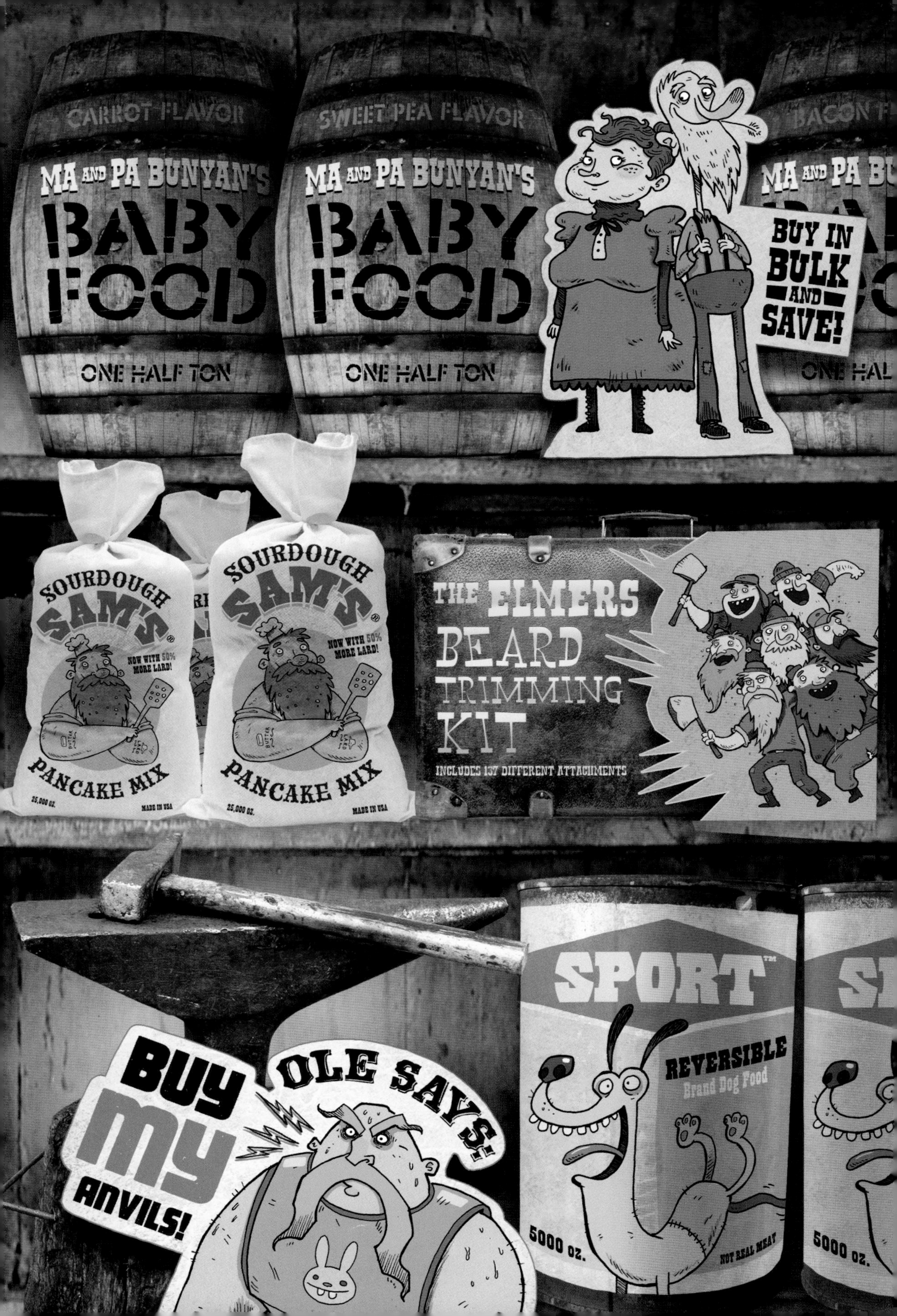
CARROT FLAVOR
MA AND PA BUNYAN'S
BABY FOOD
ONE HALF TON
SWEET PEA FLAVOR
MA AND PA BUNYAN'S
BABY FOOD
ONE HALF TON
BUY IN BULK AND SAVE!
SOURDOUGH SAM'S®
NOW WITH 50% MORE LARD!
PANCAKE MIX
25,000 OZ.
MADE IN USA
THE ELMERS BEARD TRIMMING KIT
INCLUDES 137 DIFFERENT ATTACHMENTS
SPORT™
REVERSIBLE
Brand Dog Food
5000 oz.
NOT REAL MEAT
OLE SAYS:
BUY MY ANVILS!

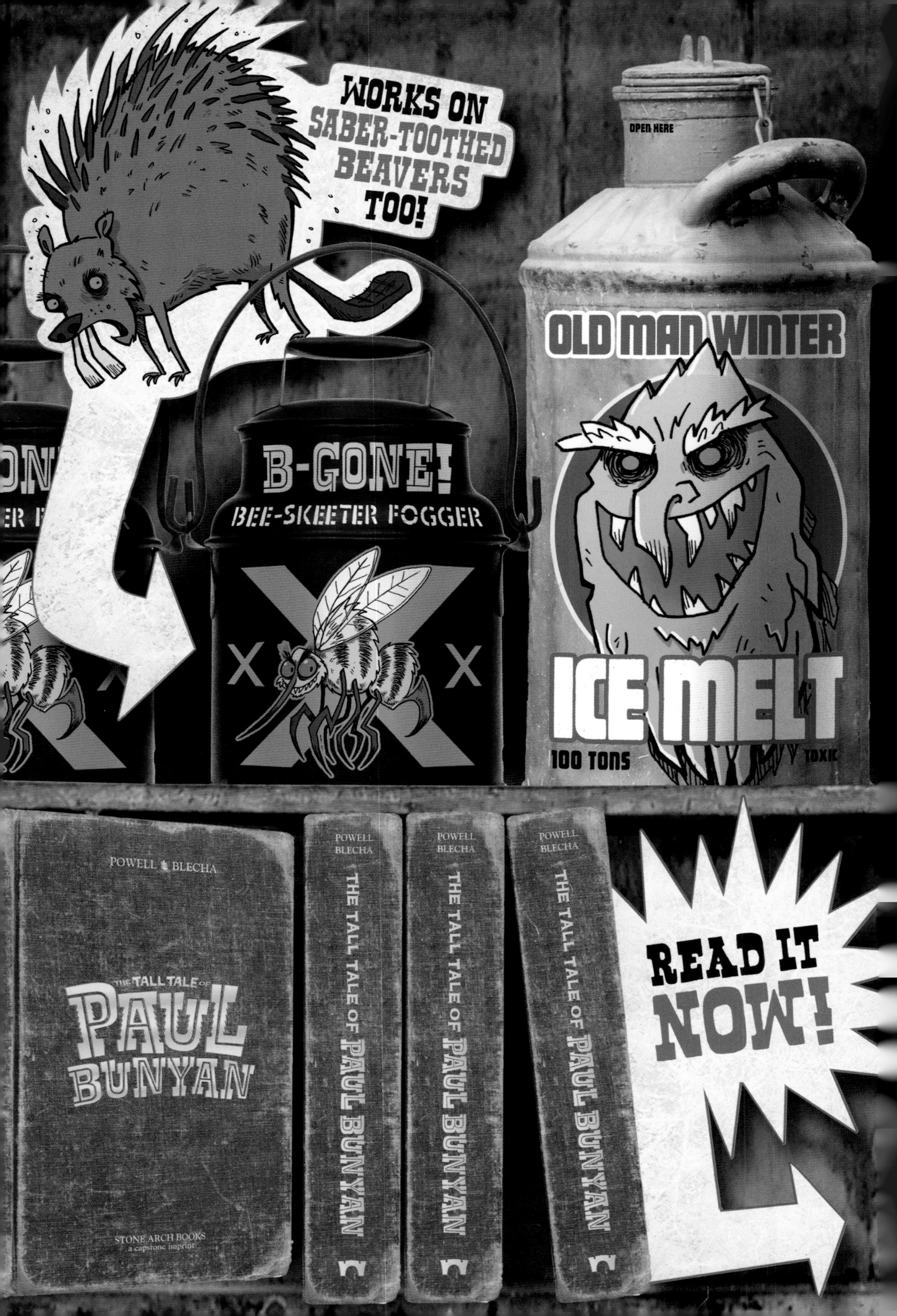
WORKS ON SABER-TOOTHED BEAVERS TOO!
OPEN HERE
OLD MAN WINTER
ICE MELT
100 TONS
TOXIC
B-GONE!
BEE-SKEETER FOGGER
POWELL BLECHA
THE TALL TALE OF PAUL BUNYAN
STONE ARCH BOOKS
a capstone imprint
POWELL
BLECHA
THE TALL TALE OF PAUL BUNYAN
POWELL
BLECHA
THE TALL TALE OF PAUL BUNYAN
POWELL
BLECHA
THE TALL TALE OF PAUL BUNYAN
READ IT NOW!

POWELL ✦ BLECHA

THE TALL TALE OF PAUL BUNYAN

STONE ARCH BOOKS
a capstone imprint

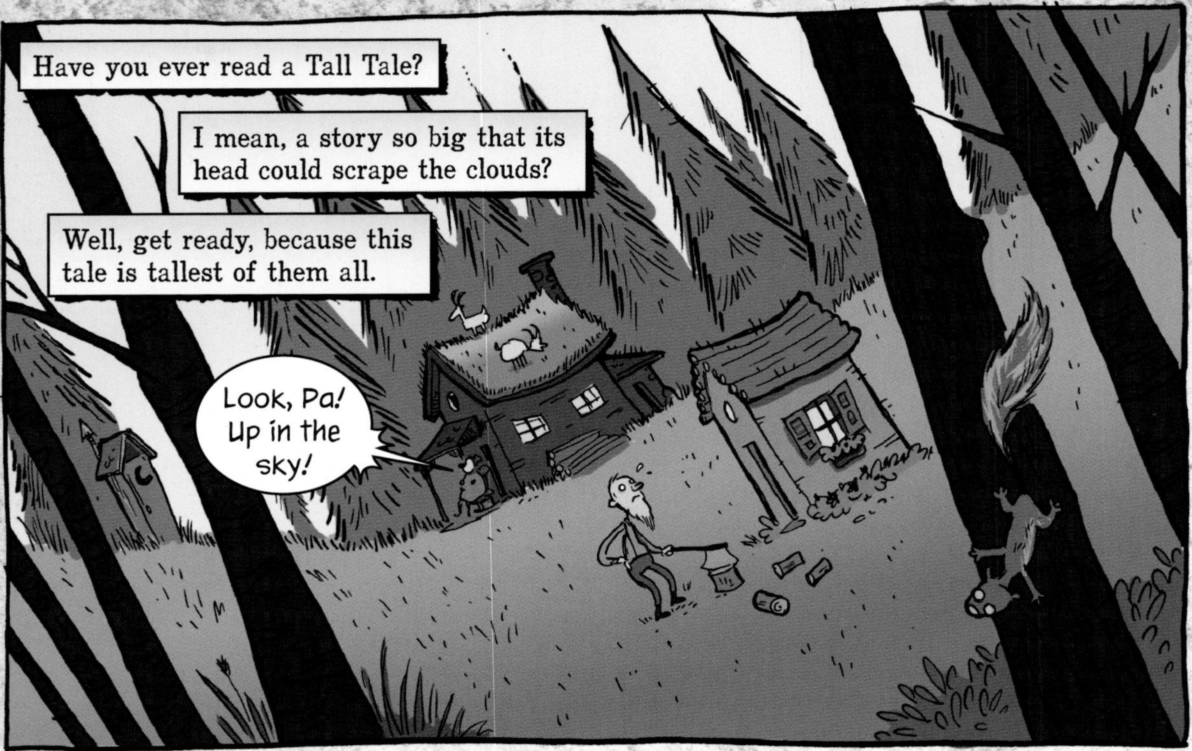
Have you ever read a Tall Tale?
I mean, a story so big that its head could scrape the clouds?
Well, get ready, because this tale is tallest of them all.
Look, Pa! Up in the sky!

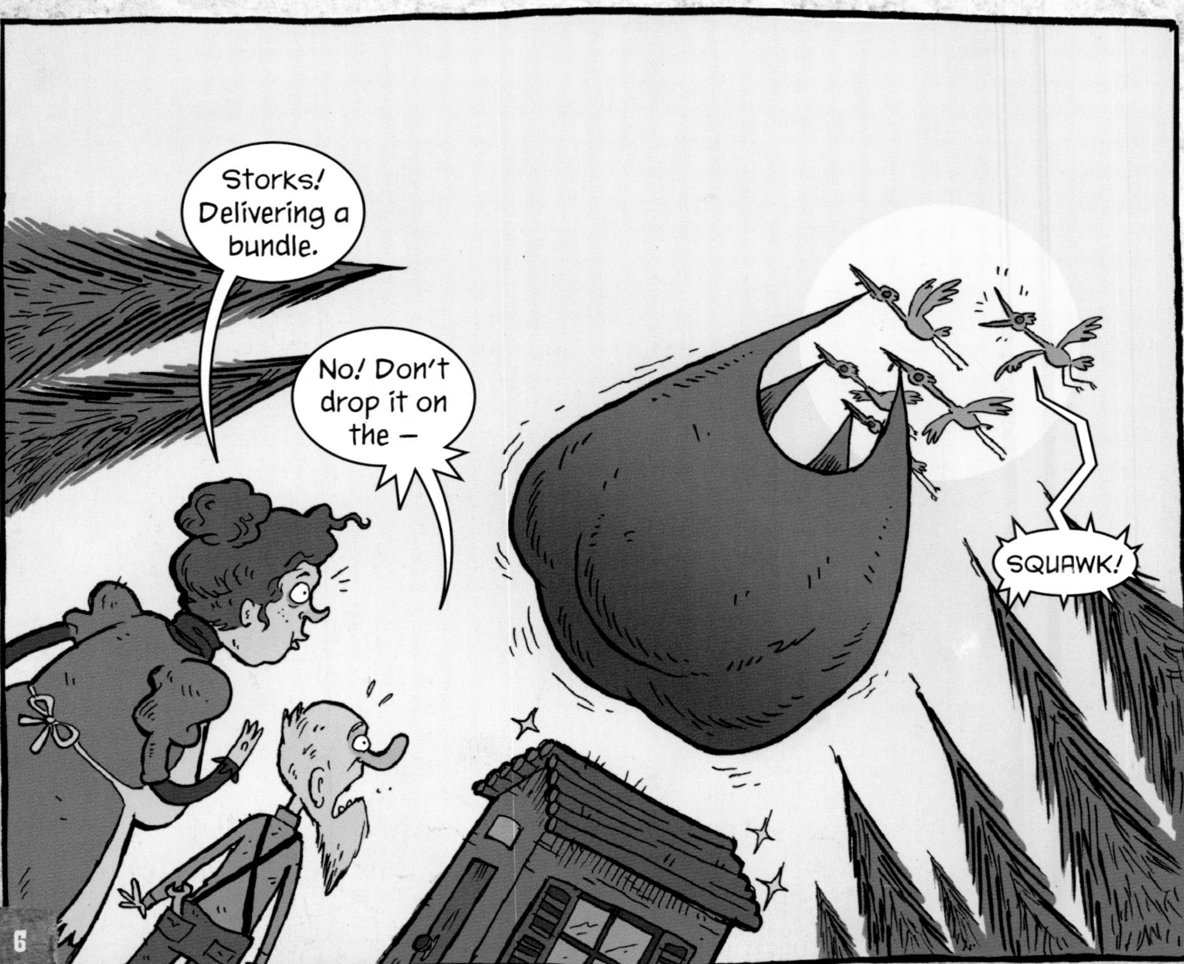
Storks! Delivering a bundle.
No! Don't drop it on the —
SQUAWK!

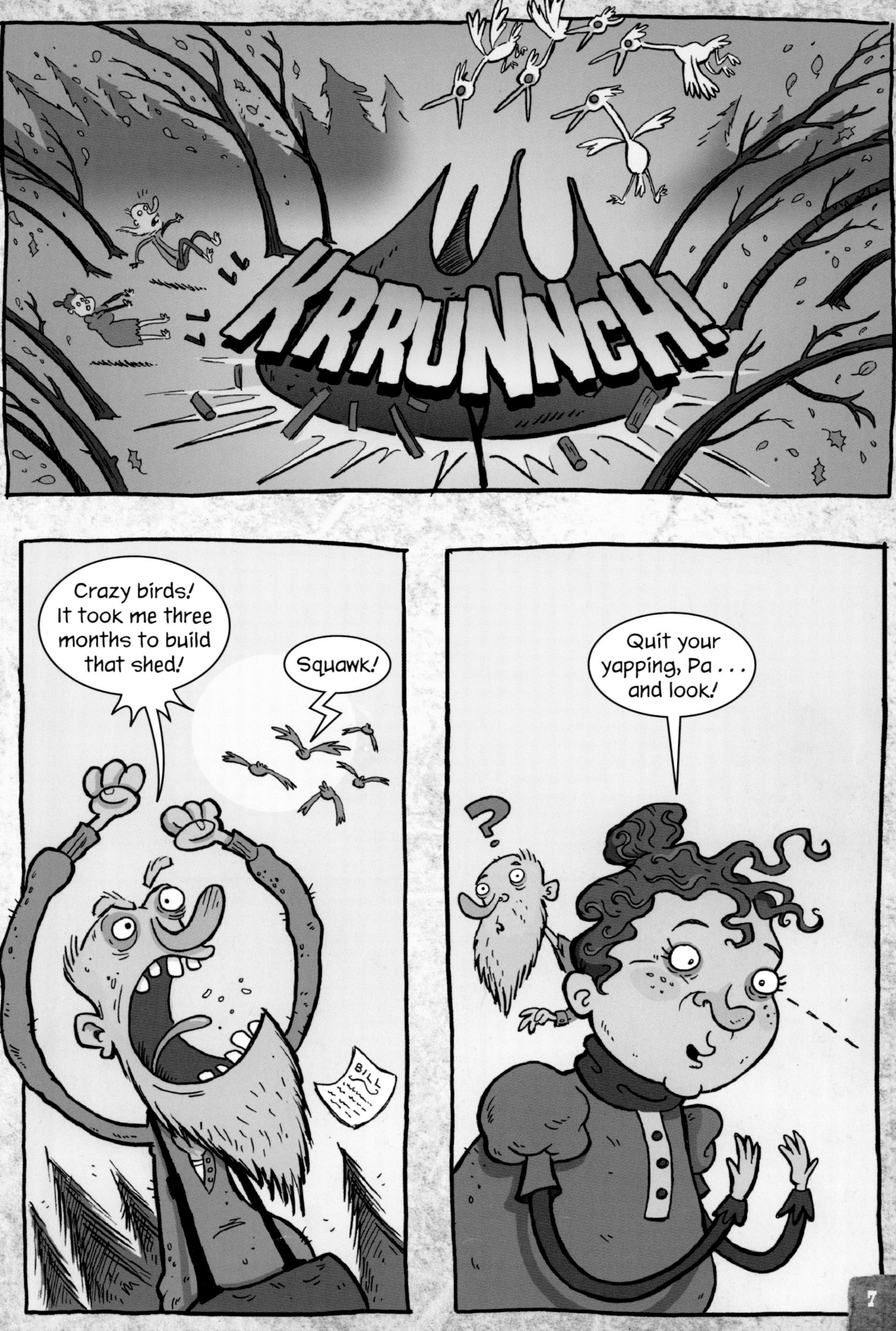
KRRUNNCH!
Crazy birds! It took me three months to build that shed!
Squawk!
BILL
Quit your yapping, Pa . . . and look!

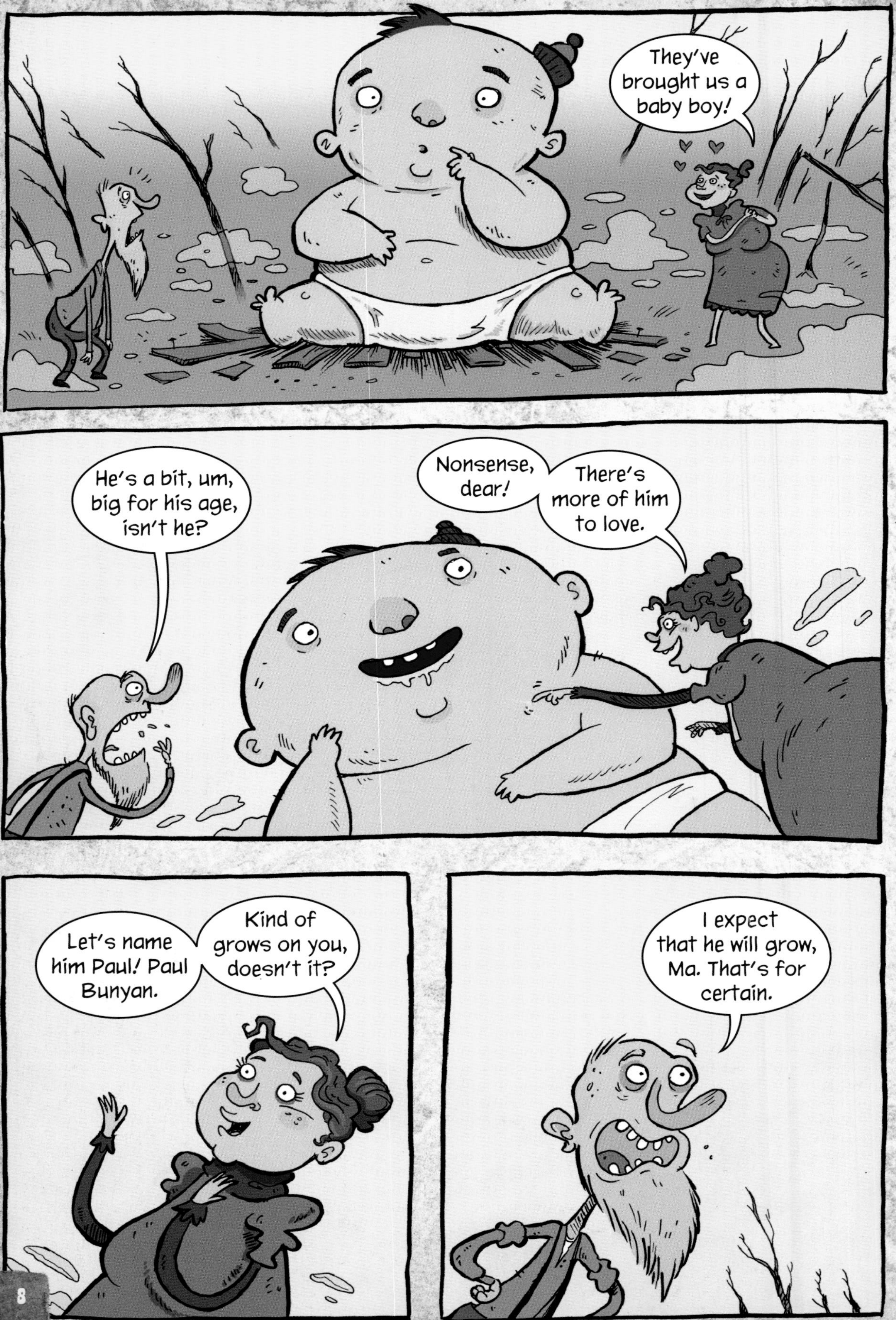
They've brought us a baby boy!
He's a bit, um, big for his age, isn't he?
Nonsense, dear!
There's more of him to love.
Let's name him Paul! Paul Bunyan.
Kind of grows on you, doesn't it?
I expect that he will grow, Ma. That's for certain.

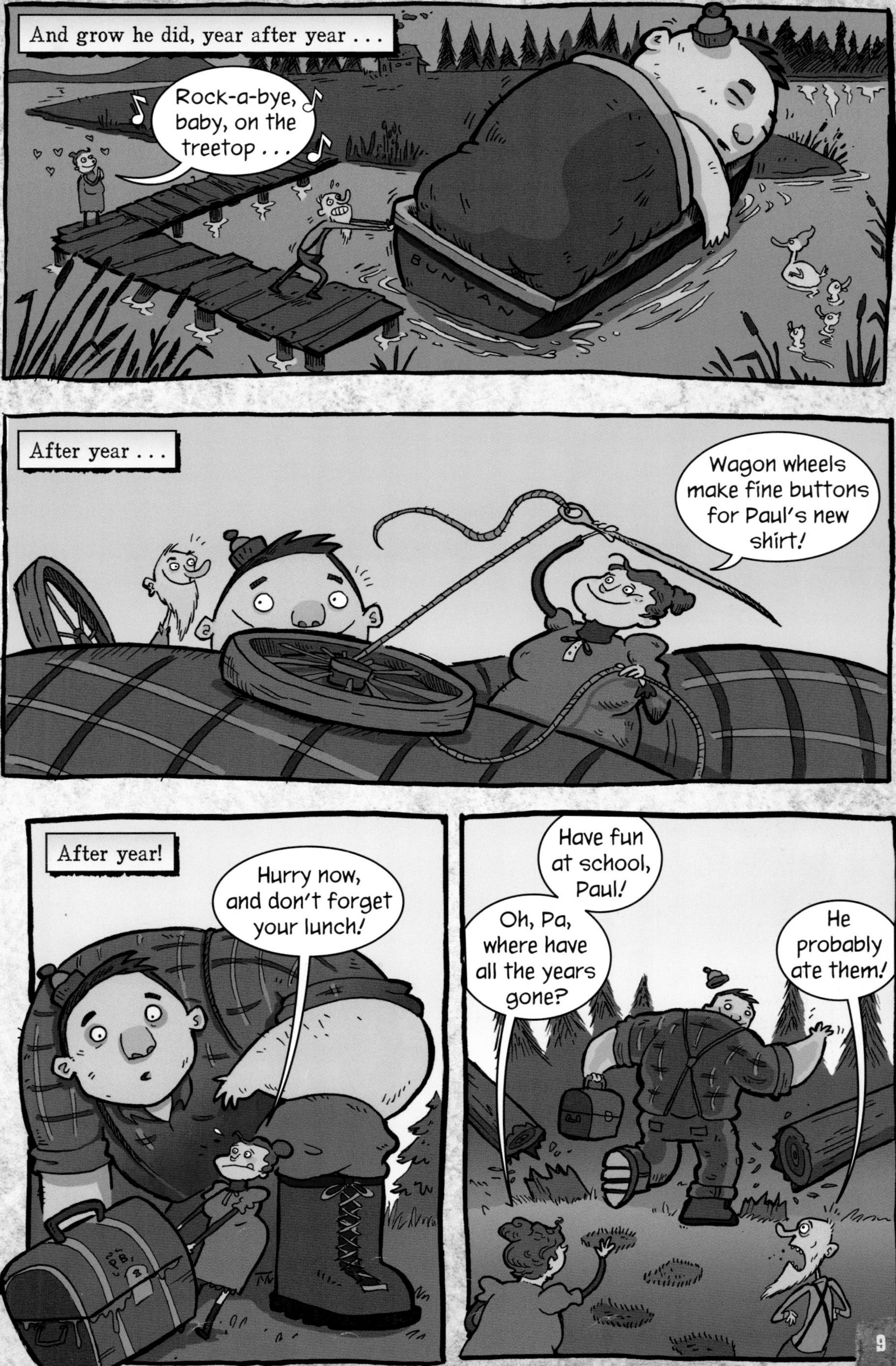
And grow he did, year after year . . .
Rock-a-bye, baby, on the treetop . . .
BUNYAN
After year . . .
Wagon wheels make fine buttons for Paul's new shirt!
After year!
Hurry now, and don't forget your lunch!
P.B.
Have fun at school, Paul!
Oh, Pa, where have all the years gone?
He probably ate them!

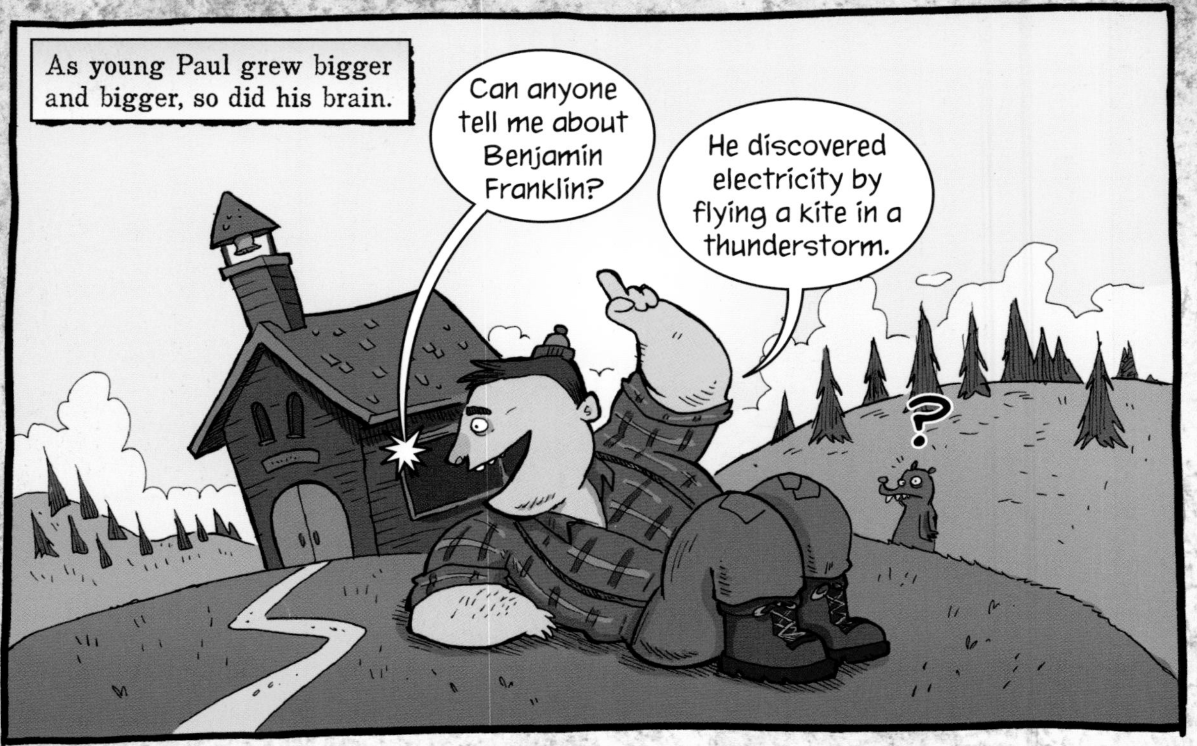
As young Paul grew bigger and bigger, so did his brain.
Can anyone tell me about Benjamin Franklin?
He discovered electricity by flying a kite in a thunderstorm.
?

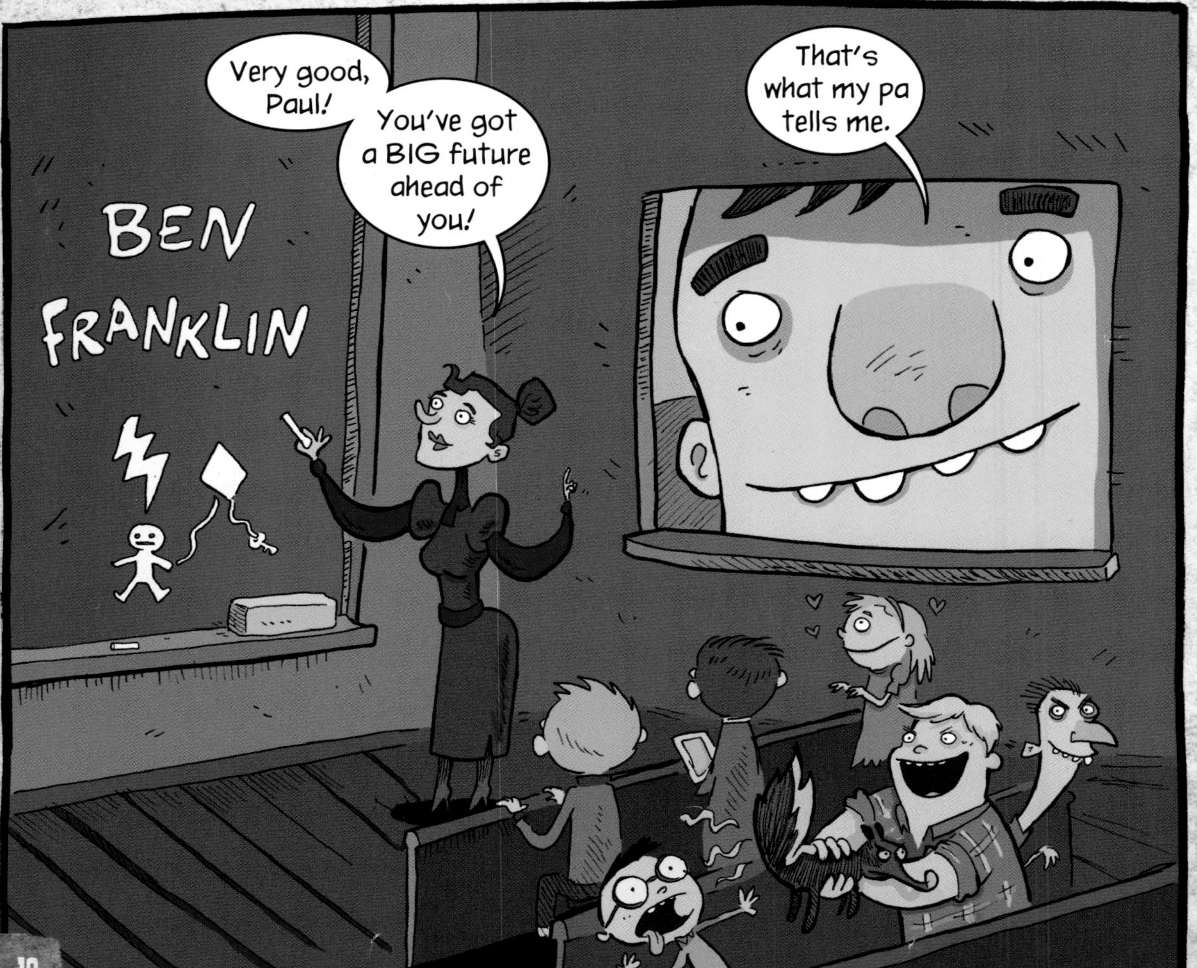
Very good, Paul!
You've got a BIG future ahead of you!
That's what my pa tells me.
BEN FRANKLIN

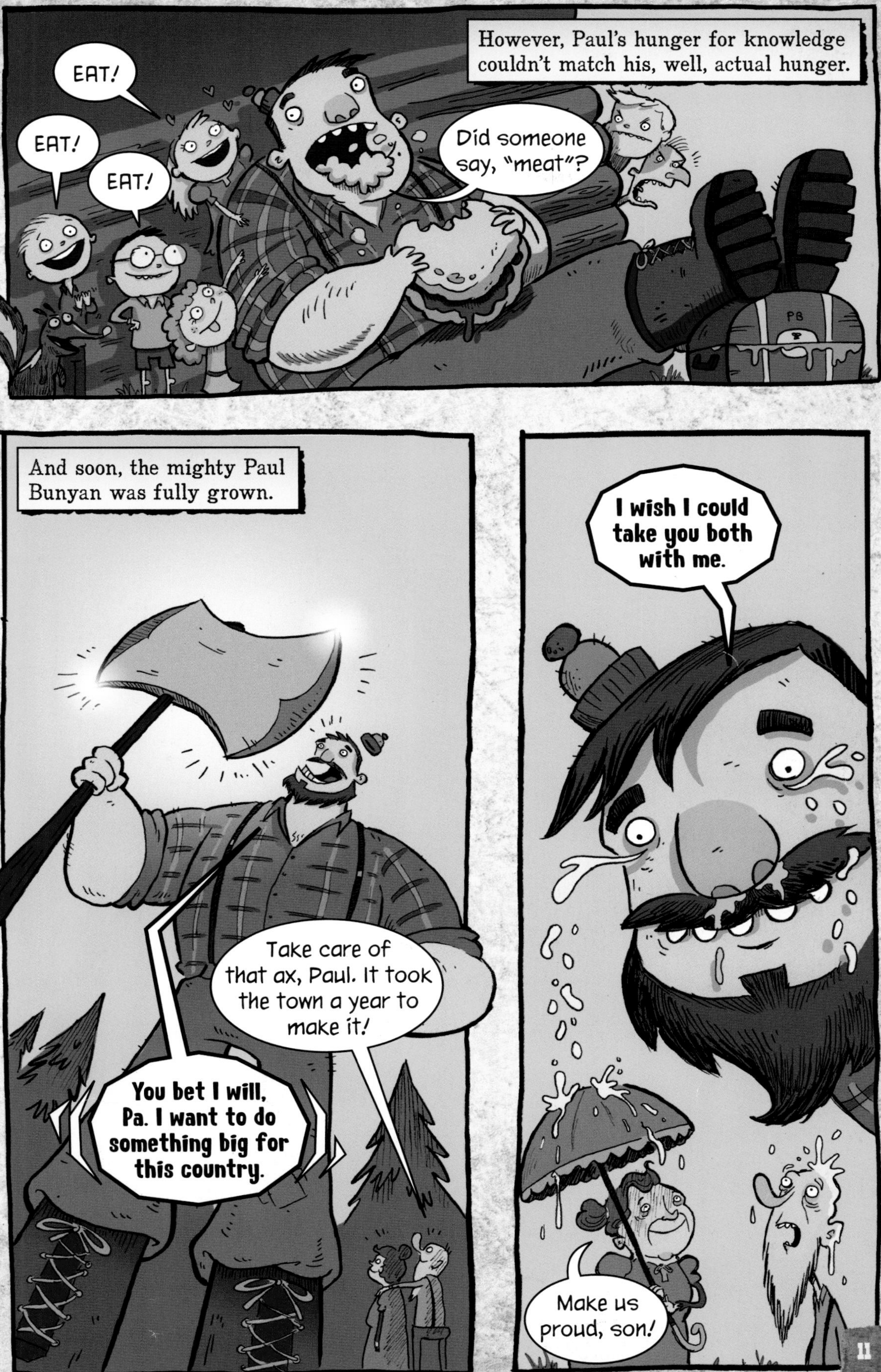

However, Paul's hunger for knowledge couldn't match his, well, actual hunger.
EAT!
EAT!
EAT!
Did someone say, "meat"?
PB
And soon, the mighty Paul Bunyan was fully grown.
Take care of that ax, Paul. It took the town a year to make it!
You bet I will, Pa. I want to do something big for this country.
I wish I could take you both with me.
Make us proud, son!

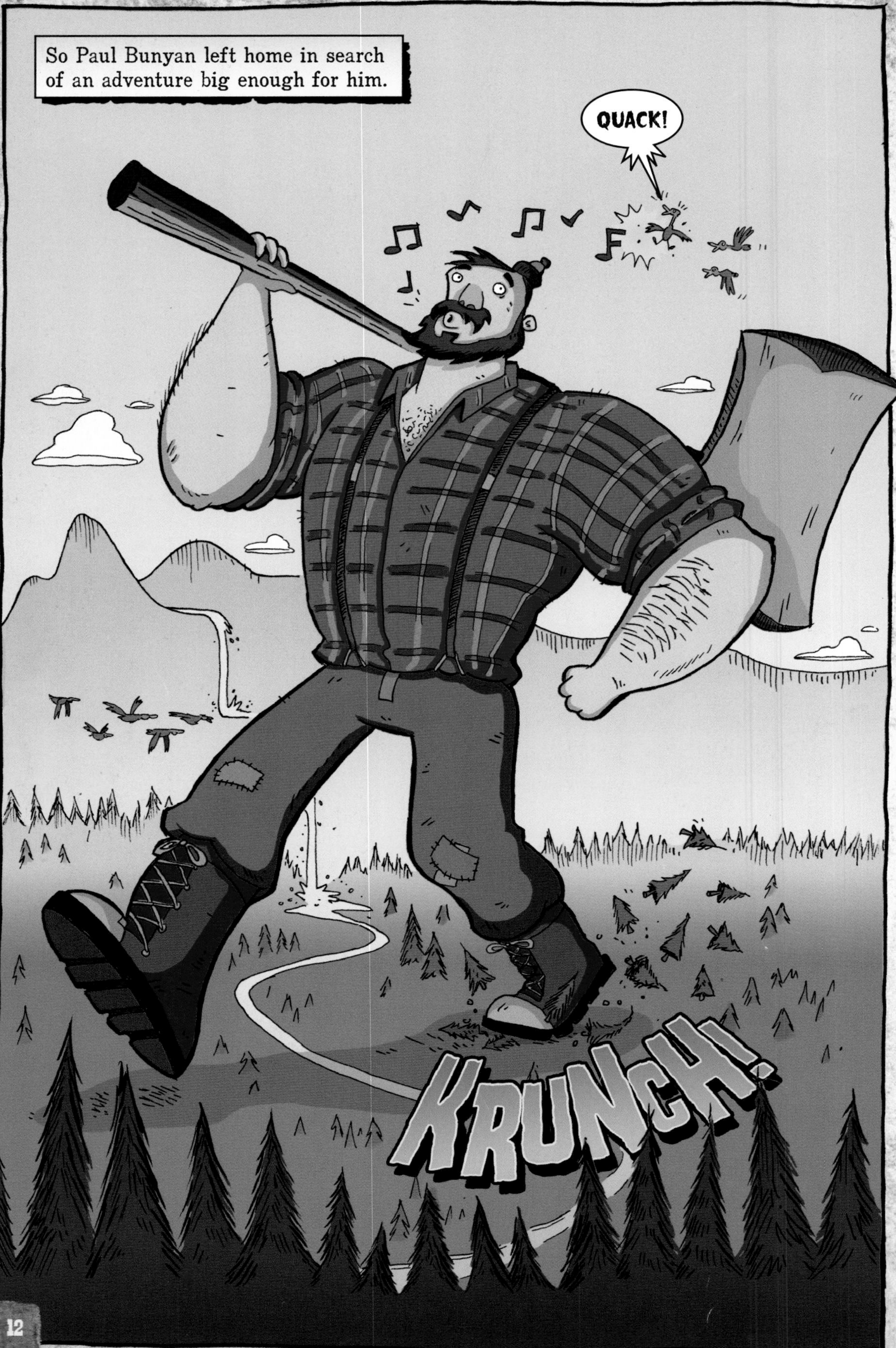
So Paul Bunyan left home in search of an adventure big enough for him.
QUACK!
KRUNCH!

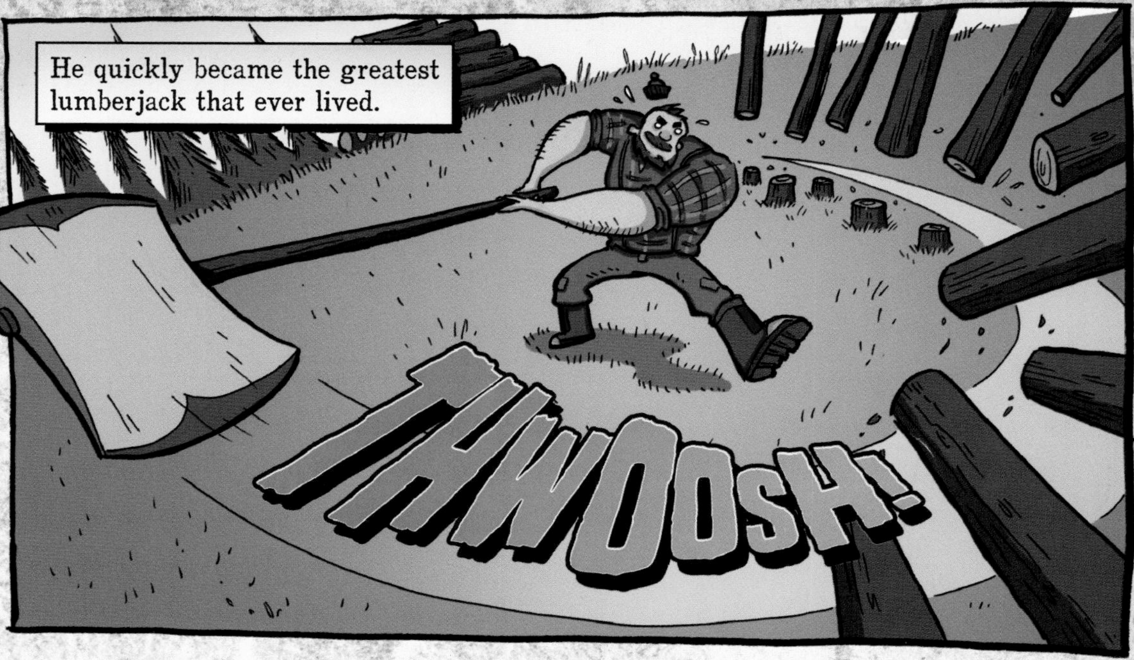
He quickly became the greatest lumberjack that ever lived.
THWOOSH!

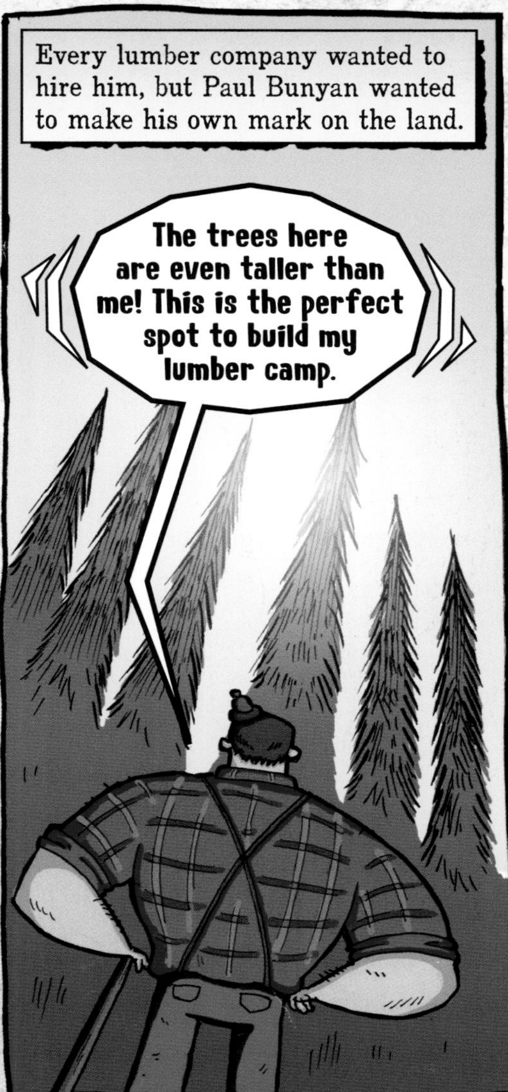
Every lumber company wanted to hire him, but Paul Bunyan wanted to make his own mark on the land.
The trees here are even taller than me! This is the perfect spot to build my lumber camp.

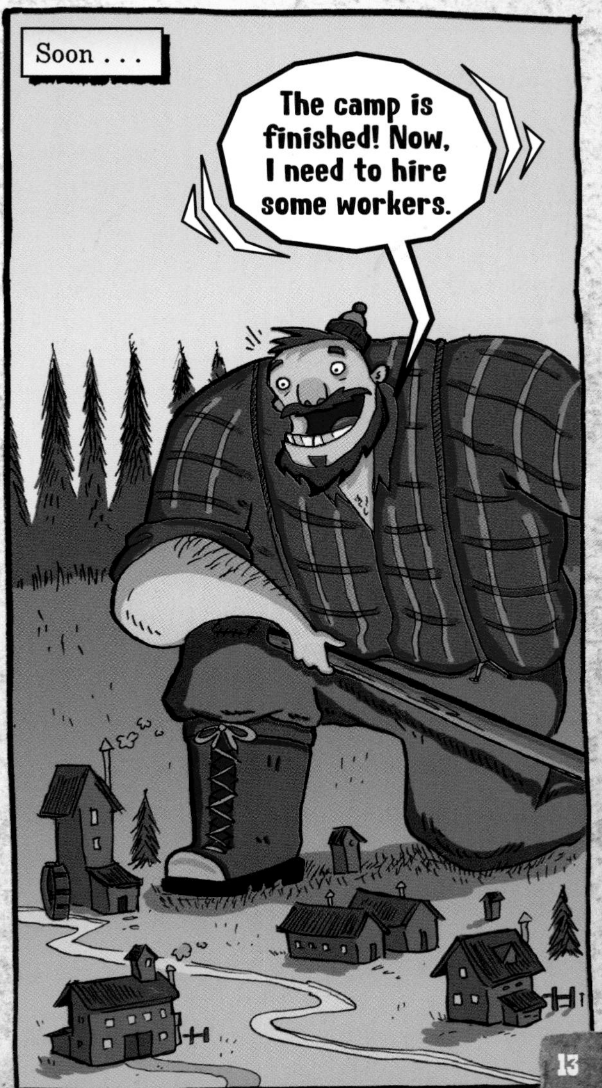
Soon . . .
The camp is finished! Now, I need to hire some workers.

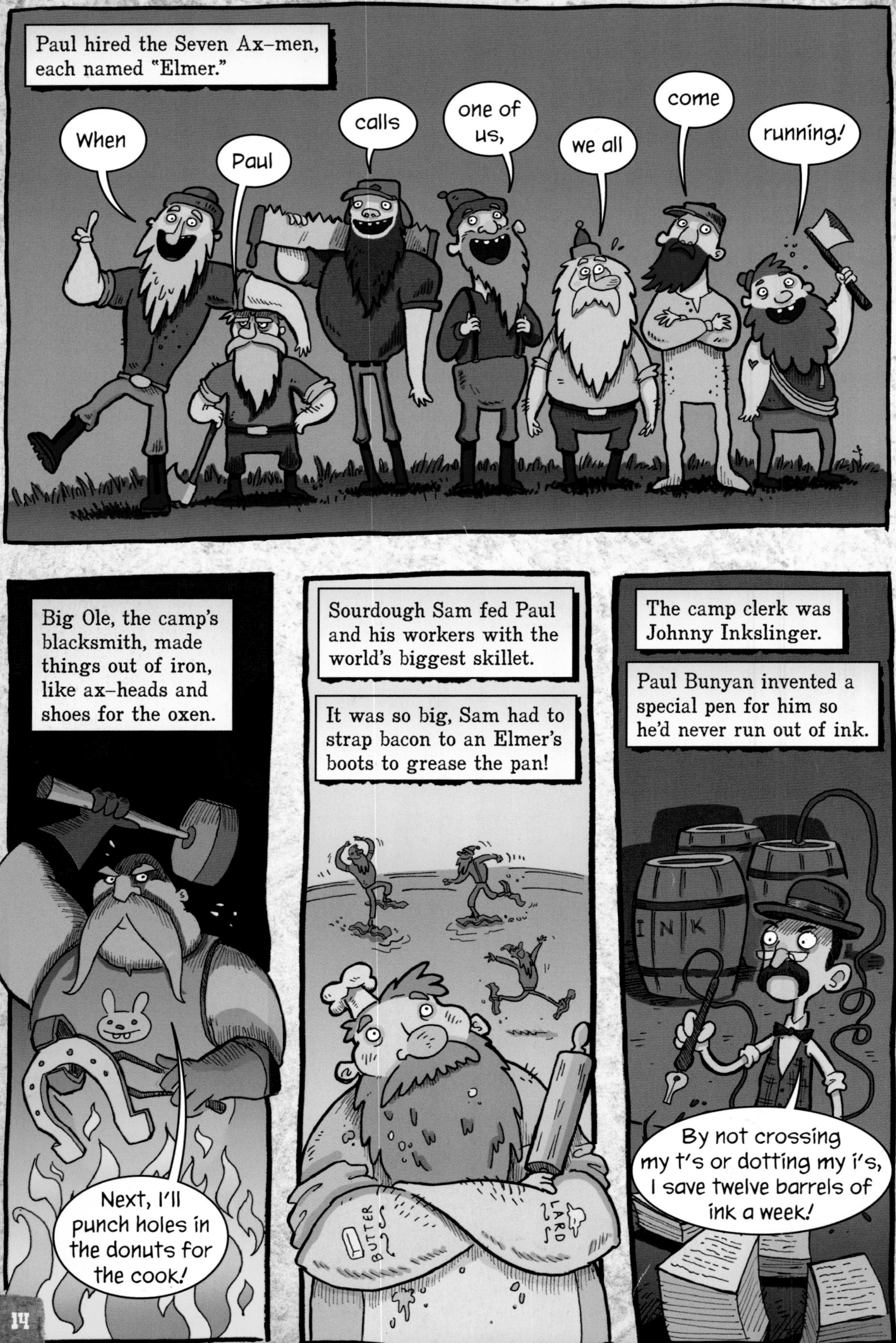

Paul hired the Seven Ax-men, each named "Elmer."
When
Paul
calls
one of us,
we all
come
running!
Big Ole, the camp's blacksmith, made things out of iron, like ax-heads and shoes for the oxen.
Next, I'll punch holes in the donuts for the cook!
Sourdough Sam fed Paul and his workers with the world's biggest skillet.
It was so big, Sam had to strap bacon to an Elmer's boots to grease the pan!
BUTTER
LARD
The camp clerk was Johnny Inkslinger.
Paul Bunyan invented a special pen for him so he'd never run out of ink.
INK
By not crossing my t's or dotting my i's, I save twelve barrels of ink a week!

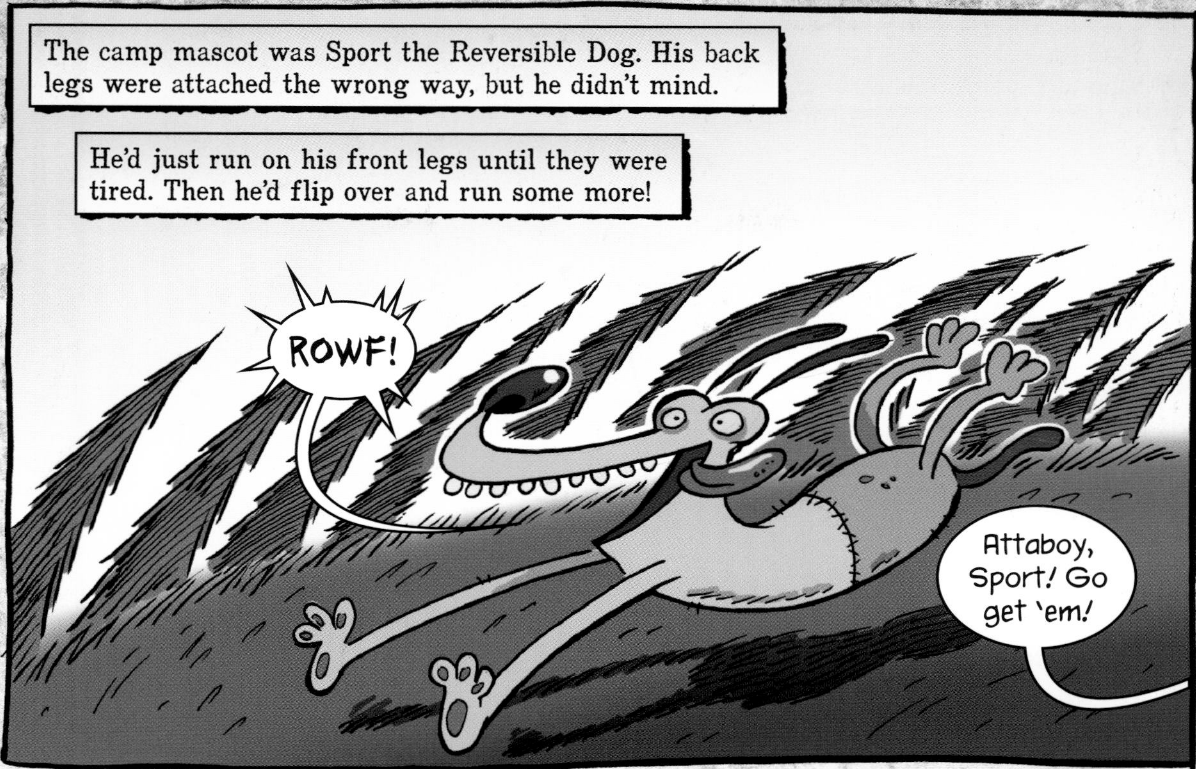
The camp mascot was Sport the Reversible Dog. His back legs were attached the wrong way, but he didn't mind.
He'd just run on his front legs until they were tired. Then he'd flip over and run some more!
ROWF!
Attaboy, Sport! Go get 'em!

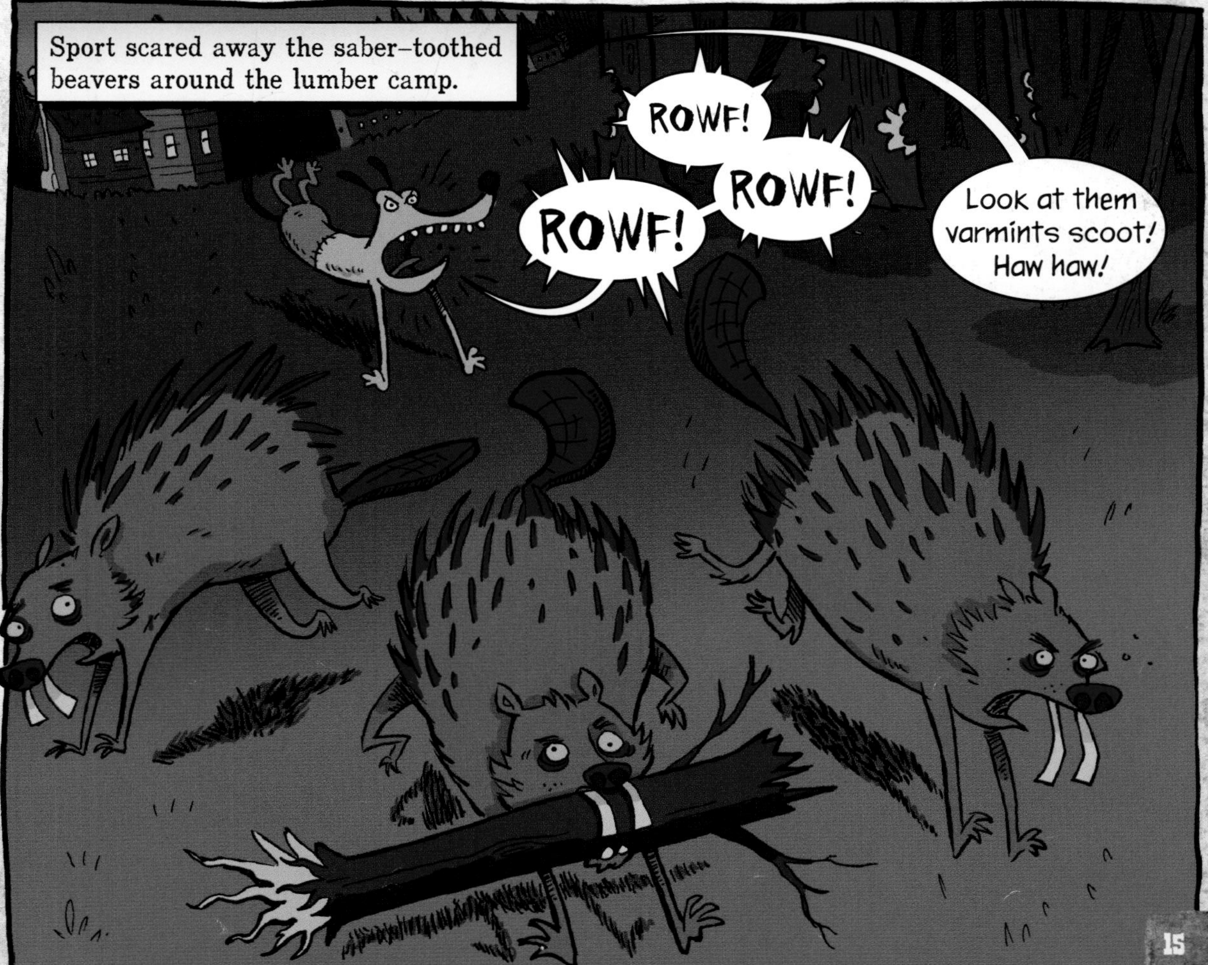
Sport scared away the saber-toothed beavers around the lumber camp.
ROWF!
ROWF!
ROWF!
Look at them varmints scoot! Haw haw!

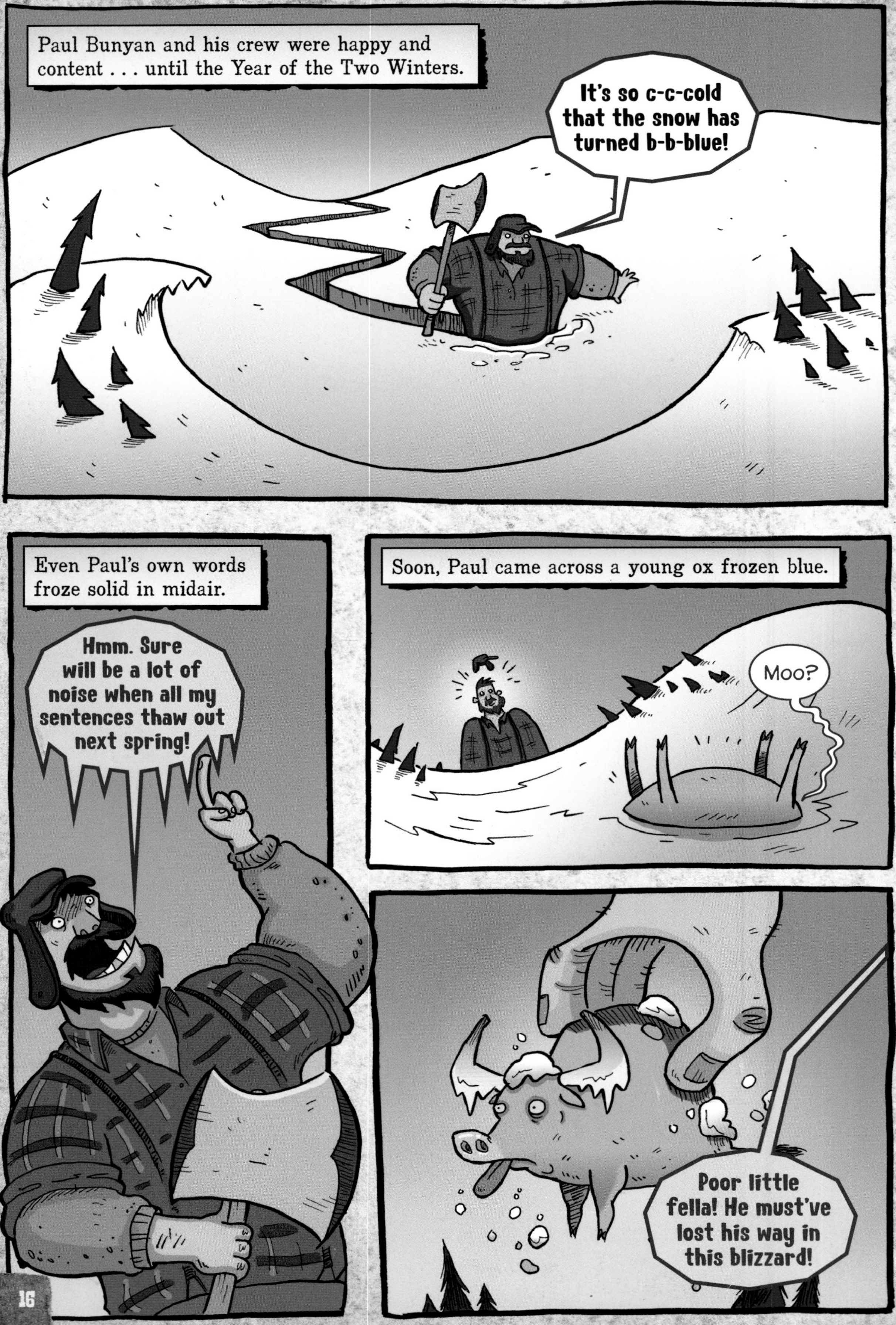
Paul Bunyan and his crew were happy and content . . . until the Year of the Two Winters.
It's so c-c-cold that the snow has turned b-b-blue!
Even Paul's own words froze solid in midair.
Hmm. Sure will be a lot of noise when all my sentences thaw out next spring!
Soon, Paul came across a young ox frozen blue.
Moo?
Poor little fella! He must've lost his way in this blizzard!

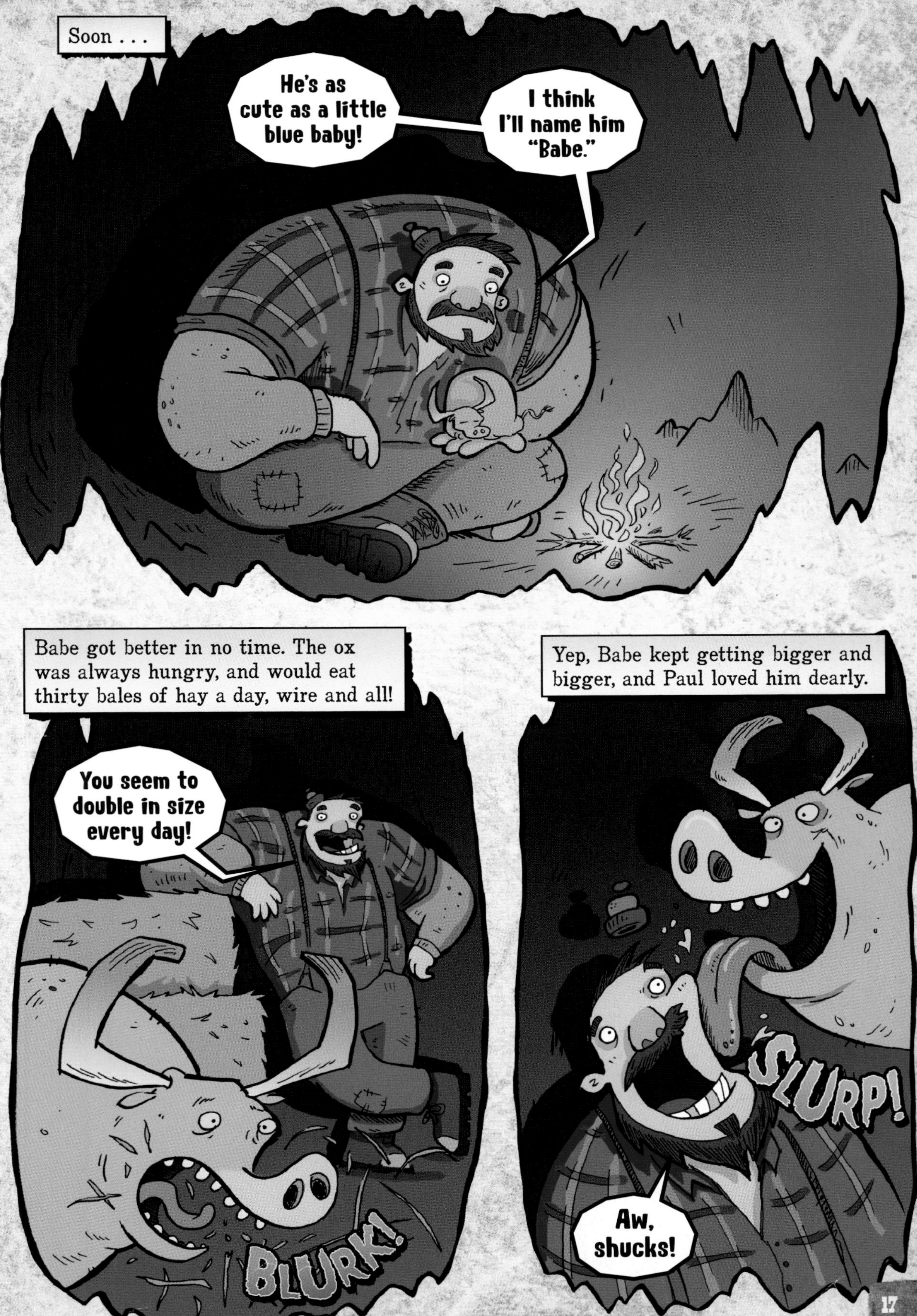
Soon . . .
He's as cute as a little blue baby!
I think I'll name him "Babe."
Babe got better in no time. The ox was always hungry, and would eat thirty bales of hay a day, wire and all!
You seem to double in size every day!
BLURK!
Yep, Babe kept getting bigger and bigger, and Paul loved him dearly.
SLURP!
Aw, shucks!

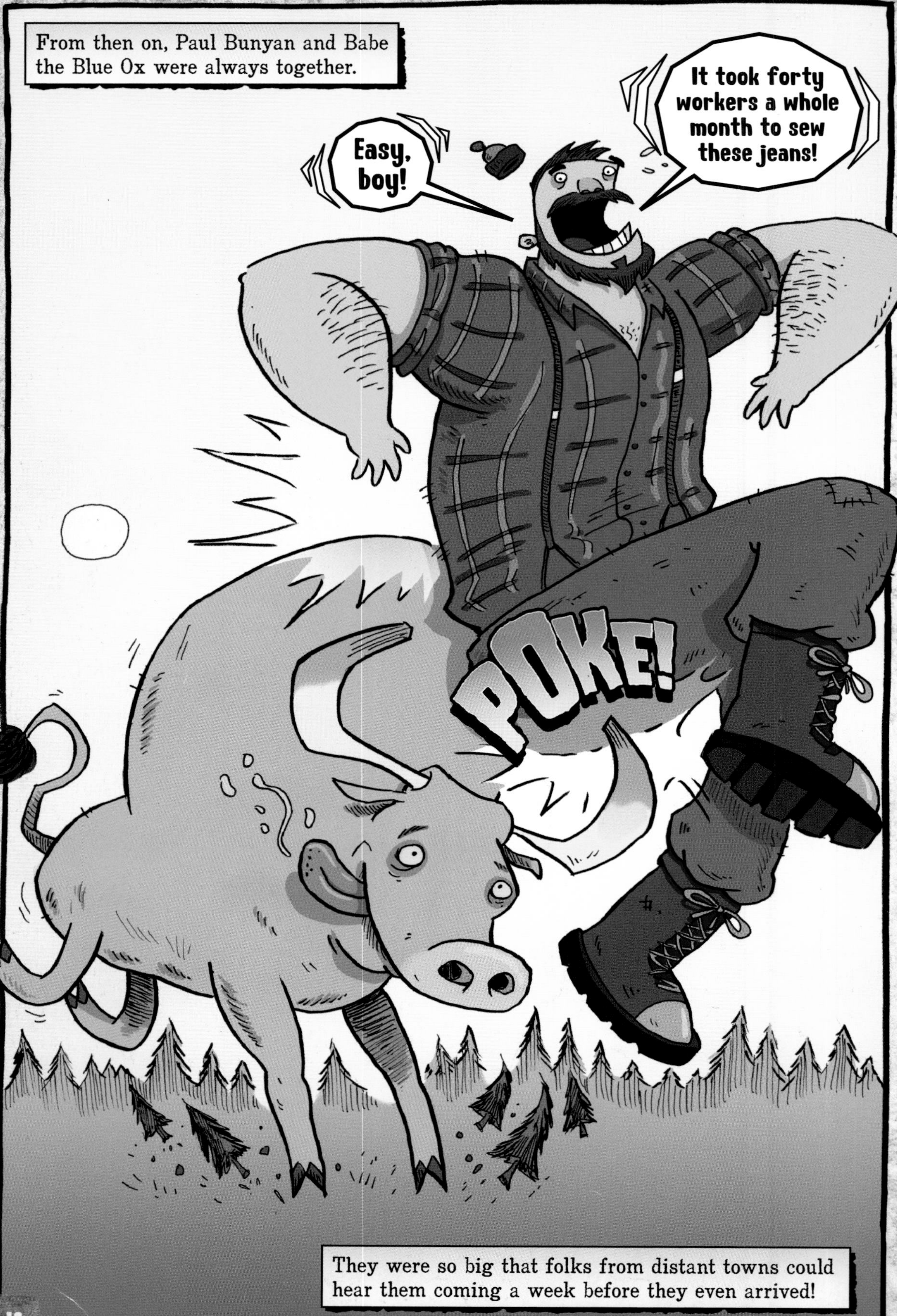
From then on, Paul Bunyan and Babe the Blue Ox were always together.
Easy, boy!
It took forty workers a whole month to sew these jeans!
POKE!
They were so big that folks from distant towns could hear them coming a week before they even arrived!

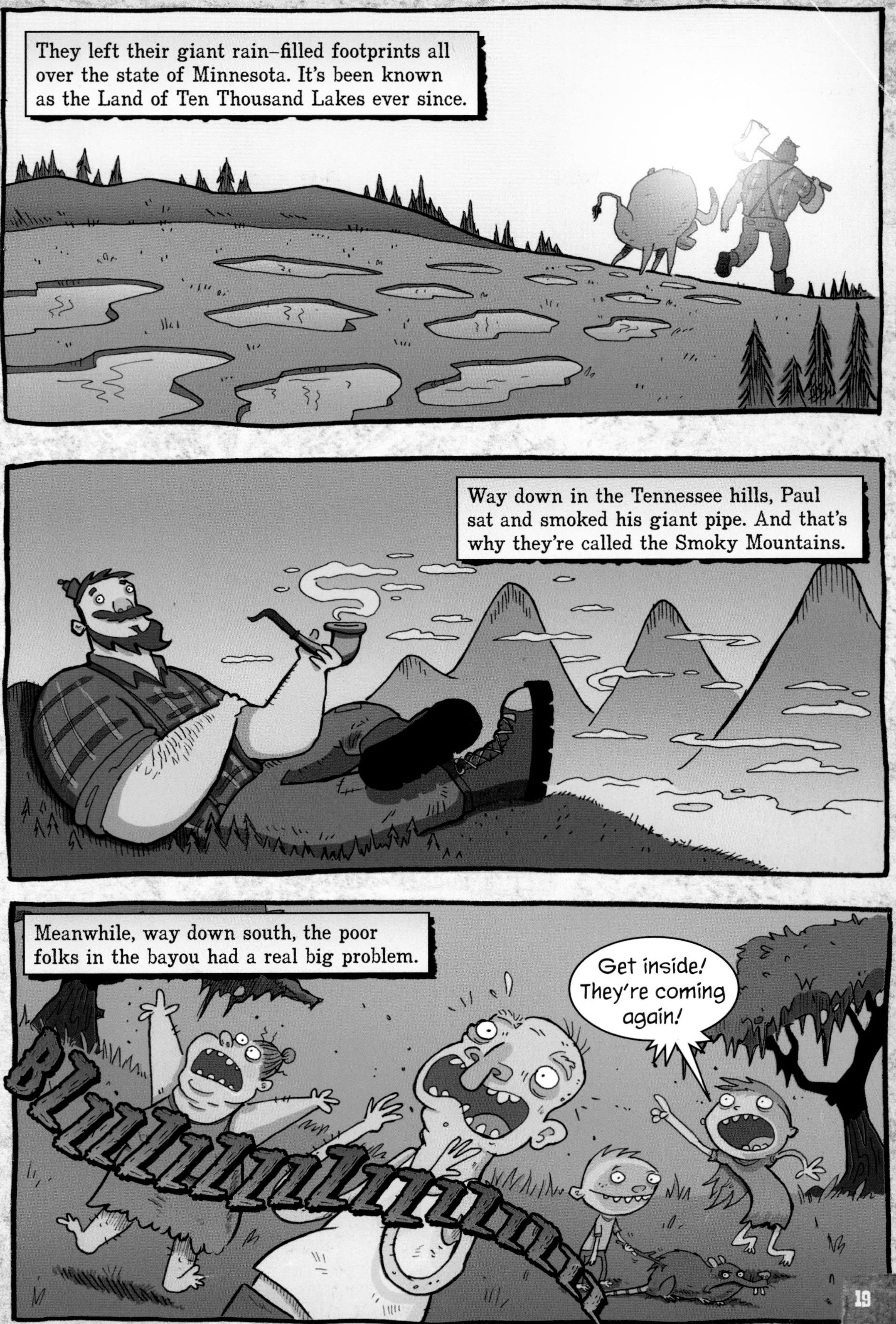
They left their giant rain–filled footprints all over the state of Minnesota. It's been known as the Land of Ten Thousand Lakes ever since.
Way down in the Tennessee hills, Paul sat and smoked his giant pipe. And that's why they're called the Smoky Mountains.
Meanwhile, way down south, the poor folks in the bayou had a real big problem.
Get inside! They're coming again!

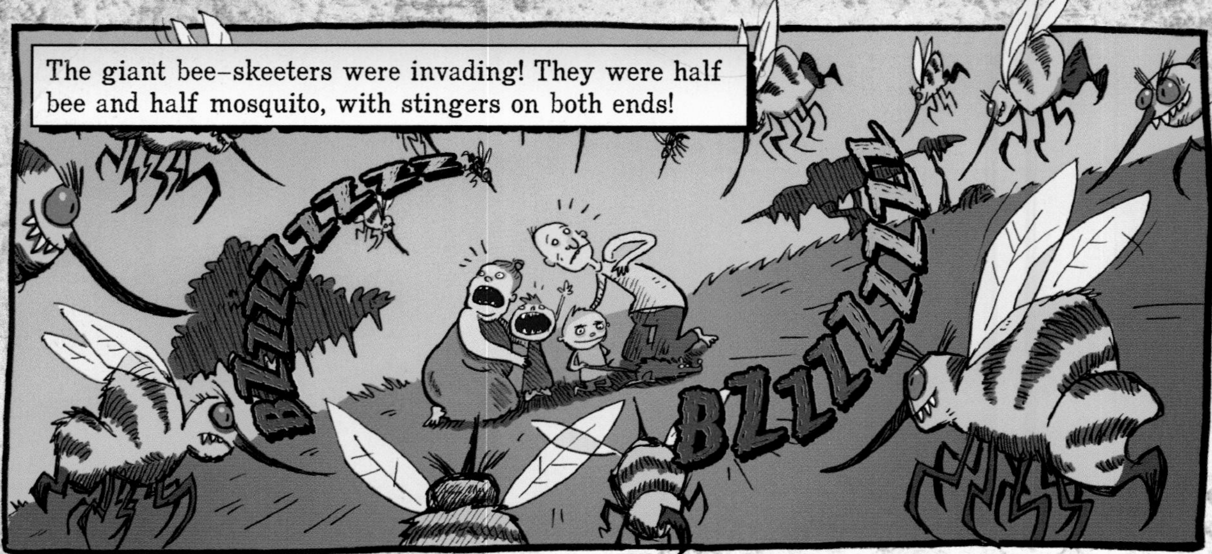
The giant bee–skeeters were invading! They were half bee and half mosquito, with stingers on both ends!

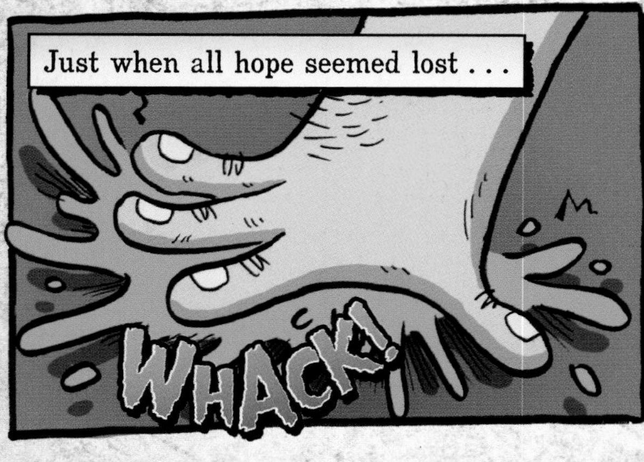
Just when all hope seemed lost . . .
WHACK!

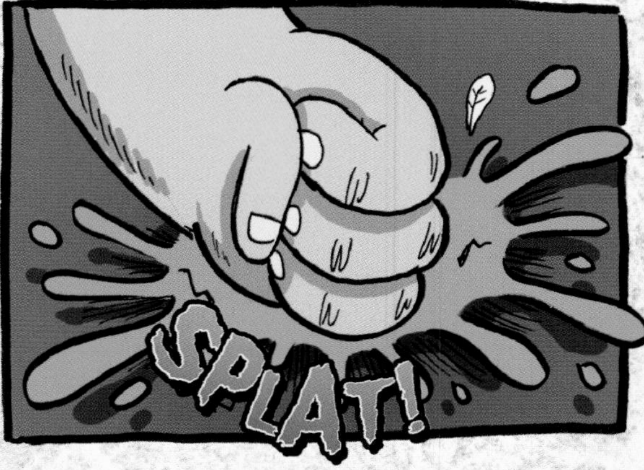
SPLAT!

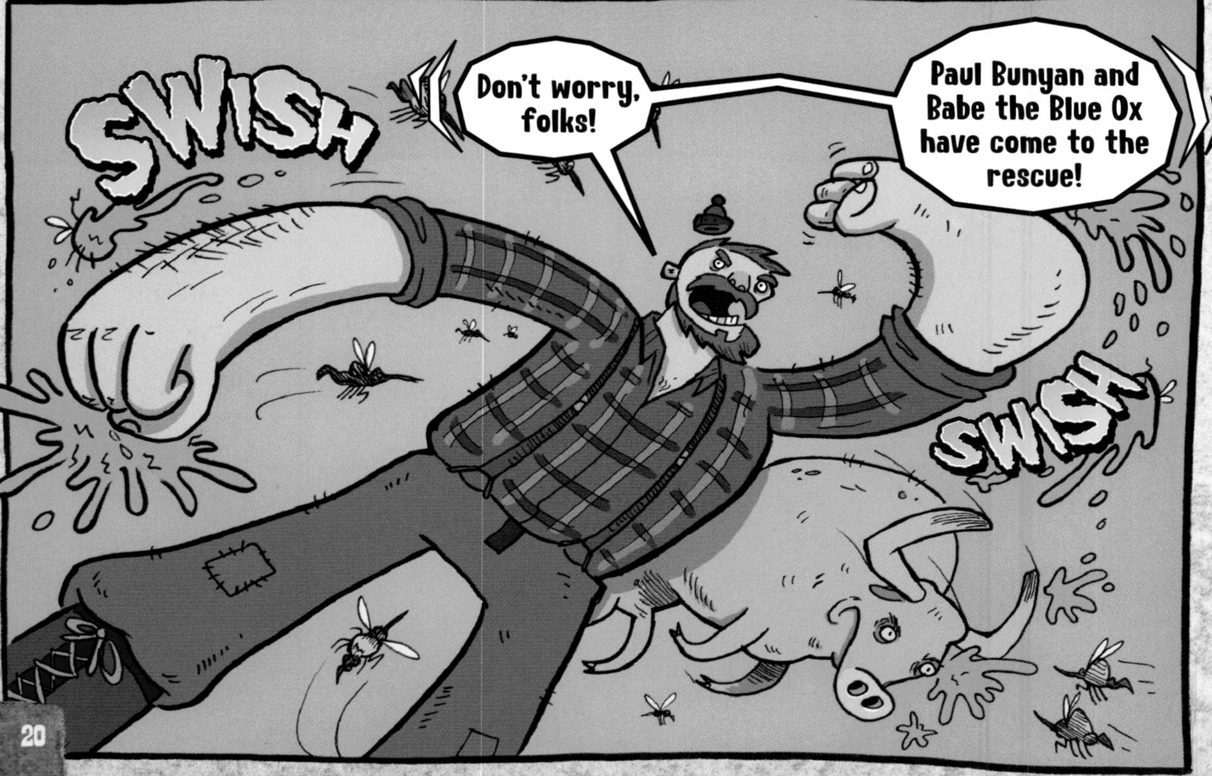
SWISH
Don't worry, folks!
Paul Bunyan and Babe the Blue Ox have come to the rescue!
SWISH

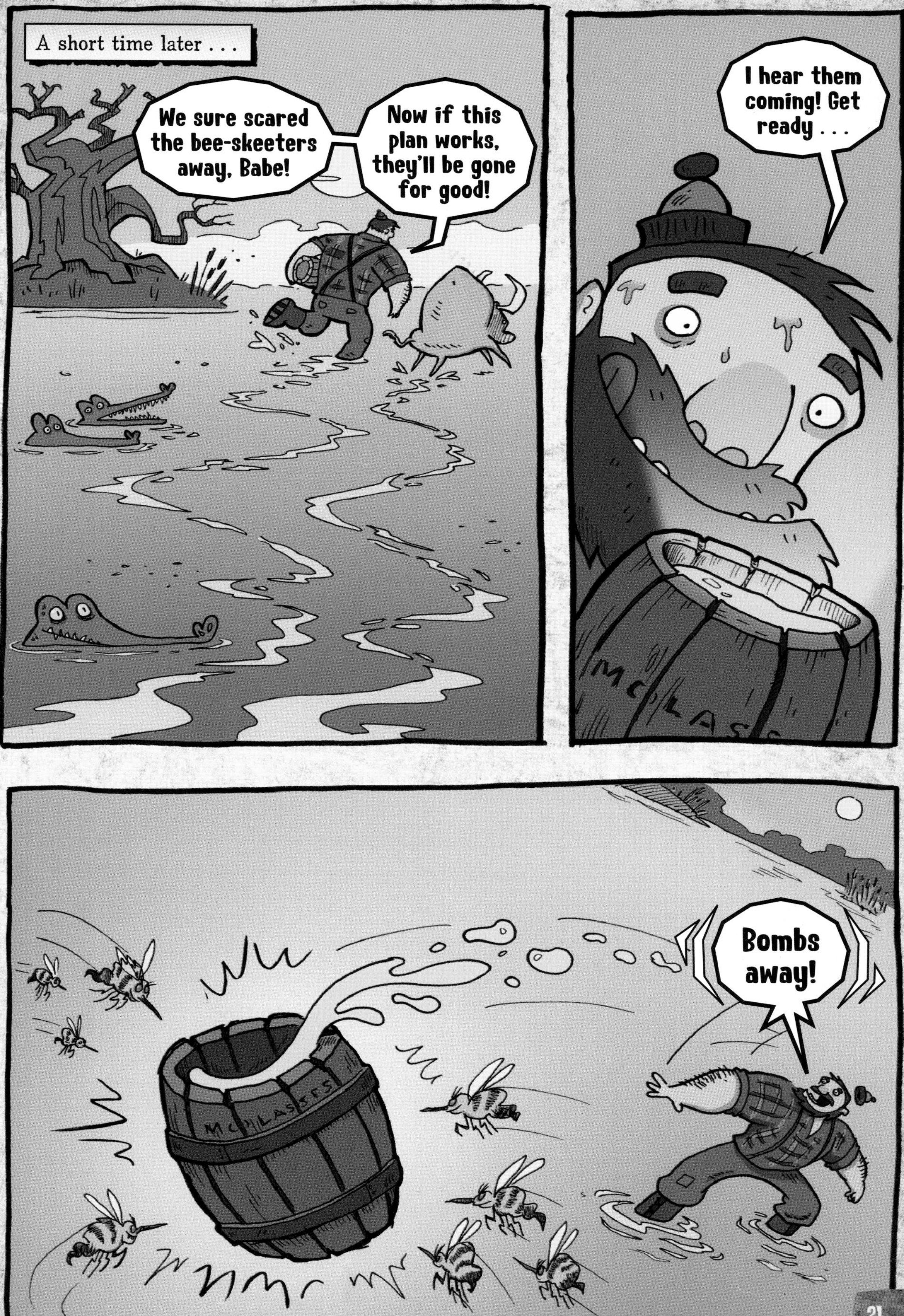
A short time later . . .
We sure scared the bee-skeeters away, Babe!
Now if this plan works, they'll be gone for good!
I hear them coming! Get ready . . .
MOLASSES
Bombs away!
MOLASSES

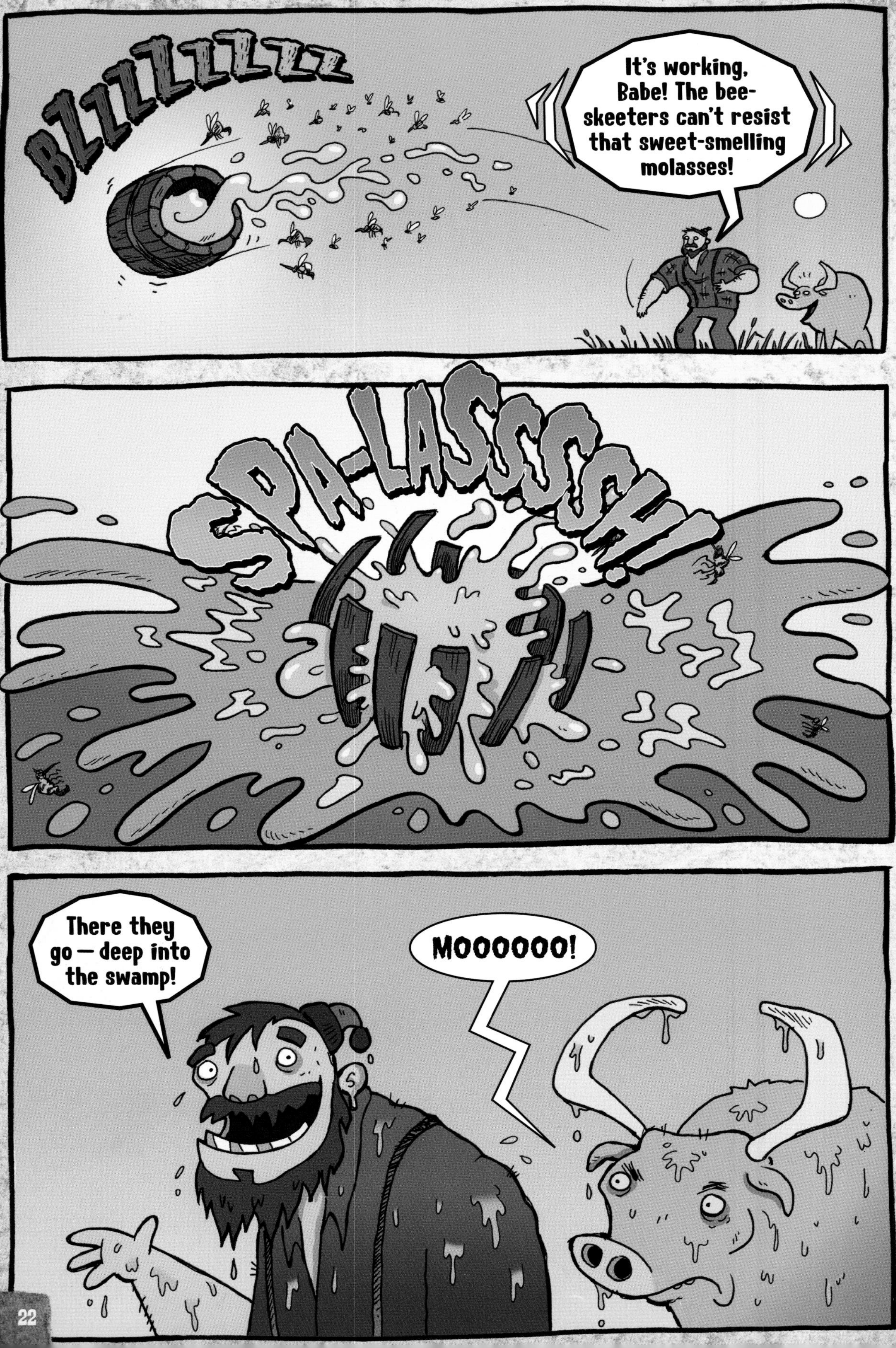
BZZZZZZZZZZ
It's working, Babe! The bee-skeeters can't resist that sweet-smelling molasses!
SPA-LASSSSH!
There they go — deep into the swamp!
MOOOOOO!

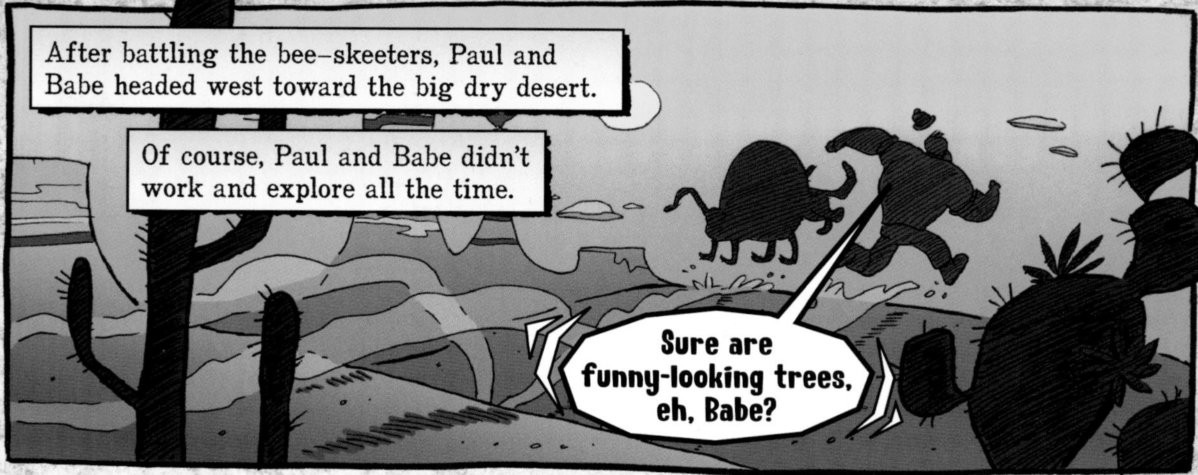
After battling the bee–skeeters, Paul and Babe headed west toward the big dry desert.
Of course, Paul and Babe didn't work and explore all the time.
Sure are funny-looking trees, eh, Babe?

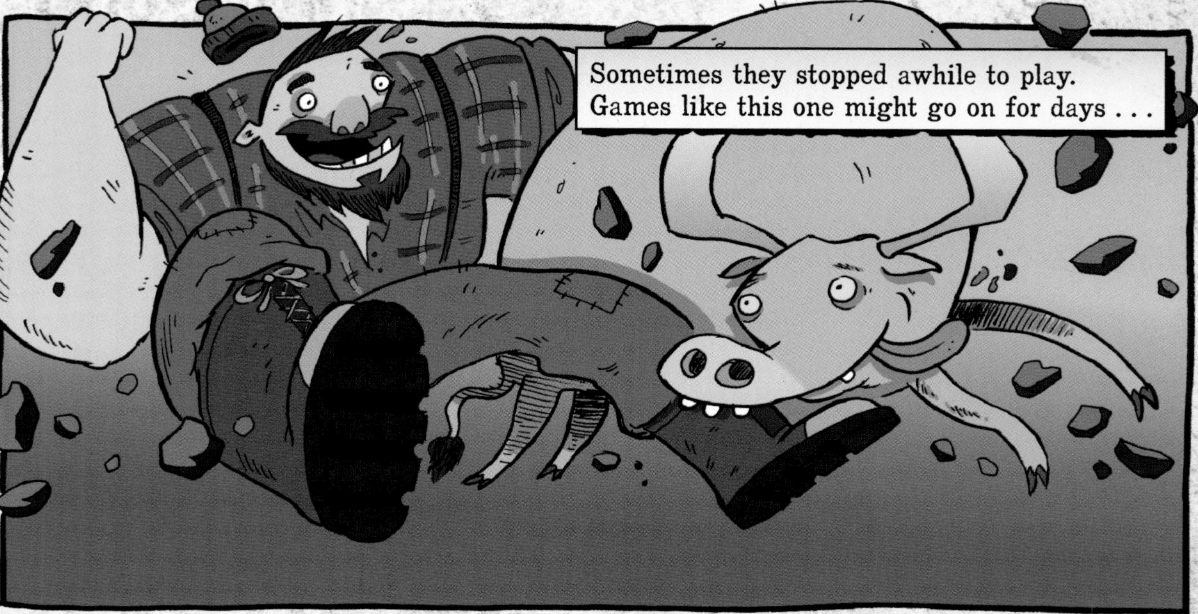
Sometimes they stopped awhile to play. Games like this one might go on for days . . .

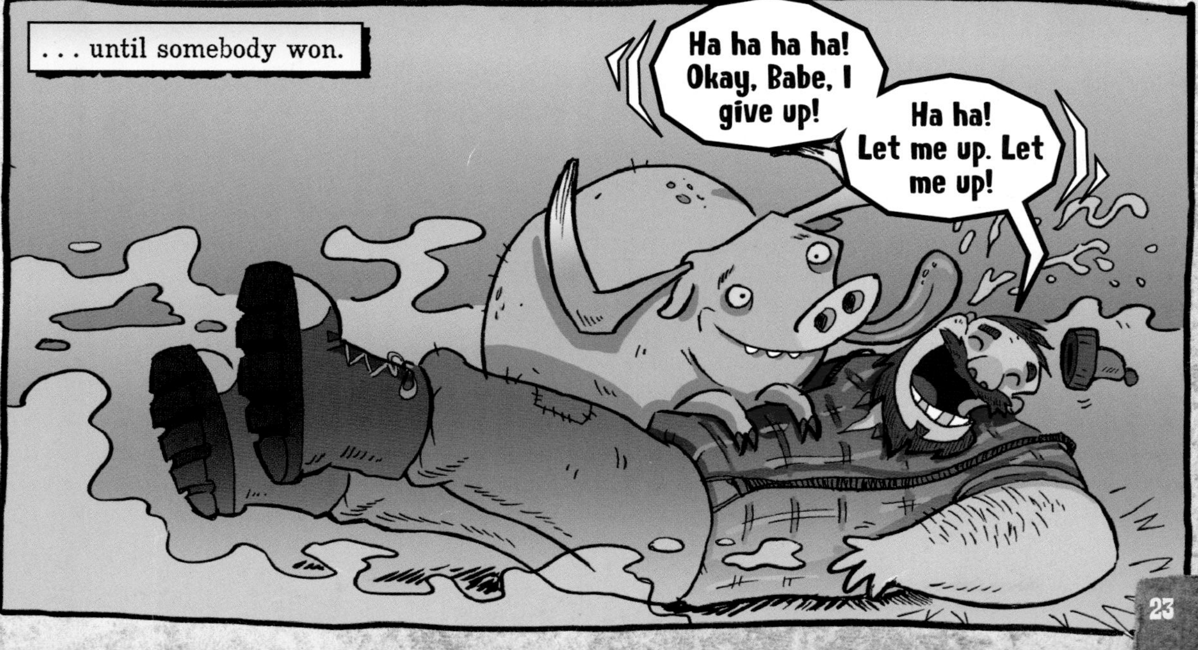
. . . until somebody won.
Ha ha ha ha! Okay, Babe, I give up!
Ha ha! Let me up. Let me up!

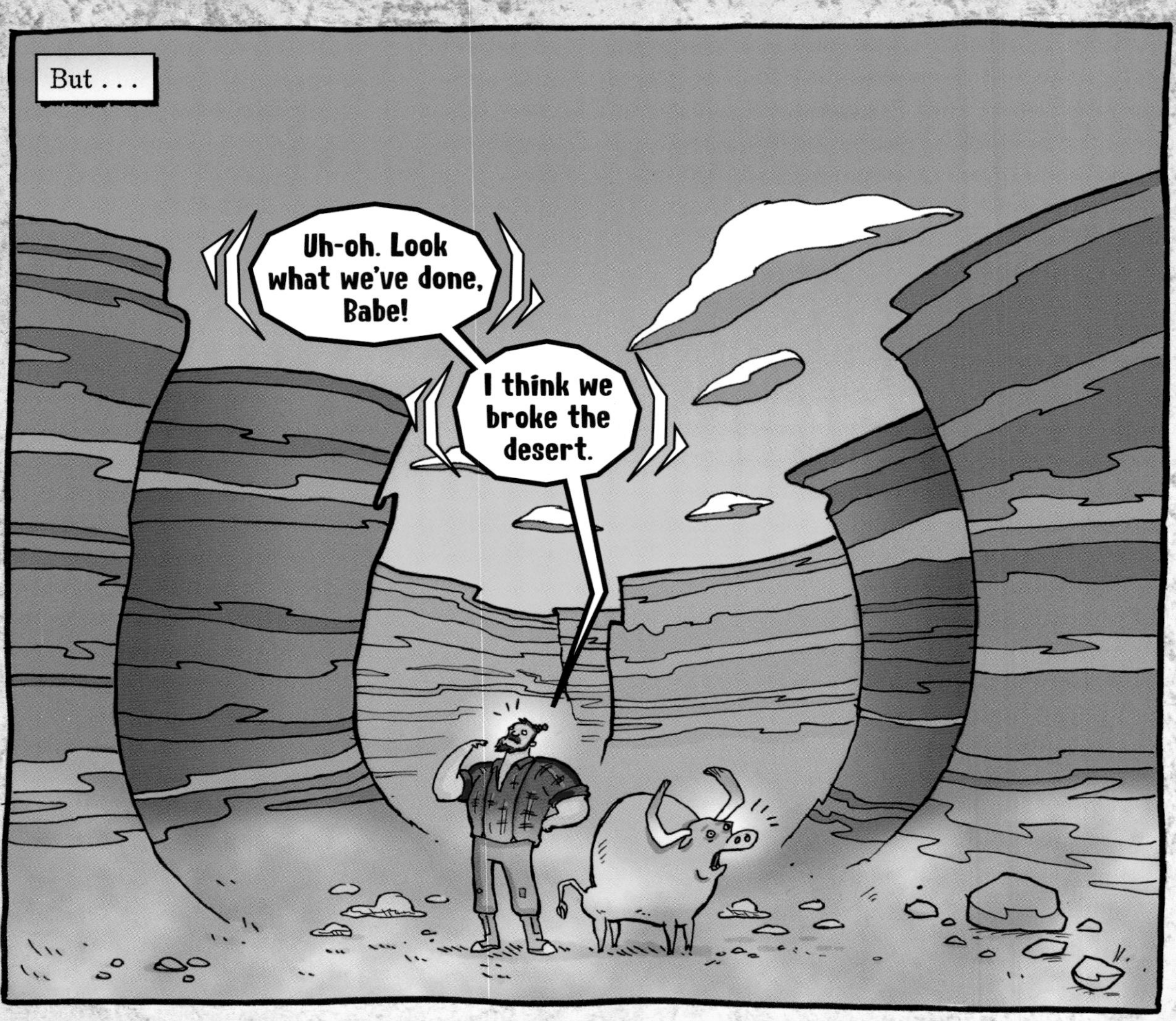
But . . .
Uh-oh. Look what we've done, Babe!
I think we broke the desert.

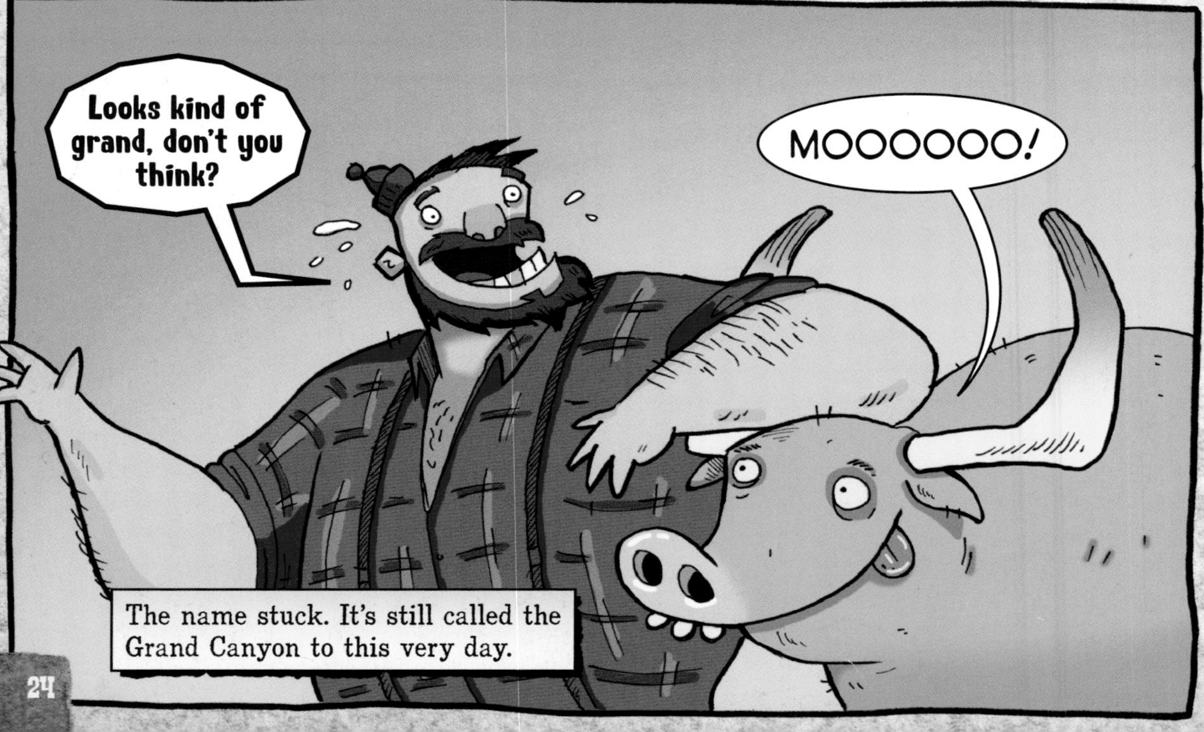
Looks kind of grand, don't you think?
MOOOOOO!
The name stuck. It's still called the Grand Canyon to this very day.

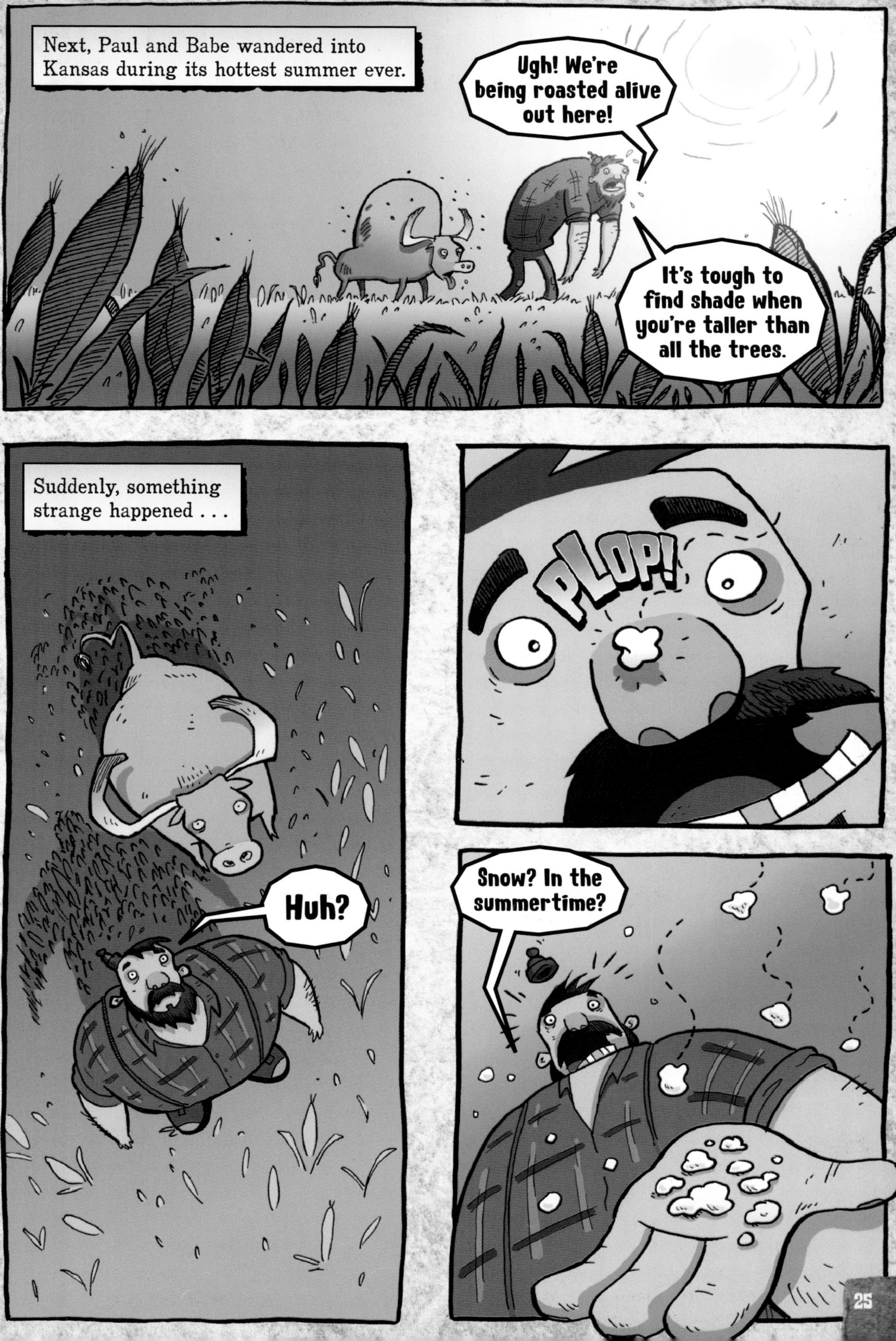
Next, Paul and Babe wandered into Kansas during its hottest summer ever.
Ugh! We're being roasted alive out here!
It's tough to find shade when you're taller than all the trees.
Suddenly, something strange happened . . .
Huh?
PLOP!
Snow? In the summertime?

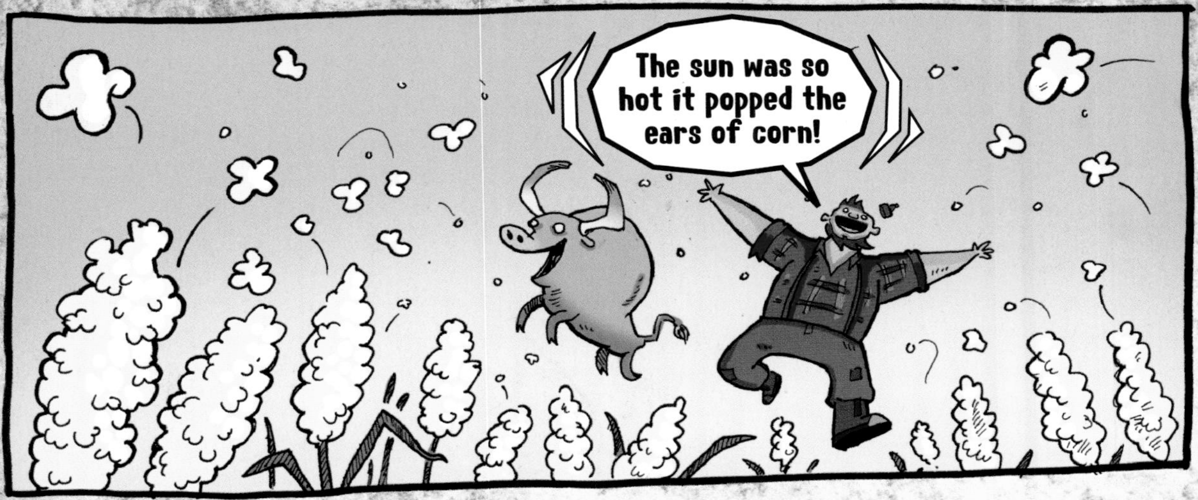
The sun was so hot it popped the ears of corn!

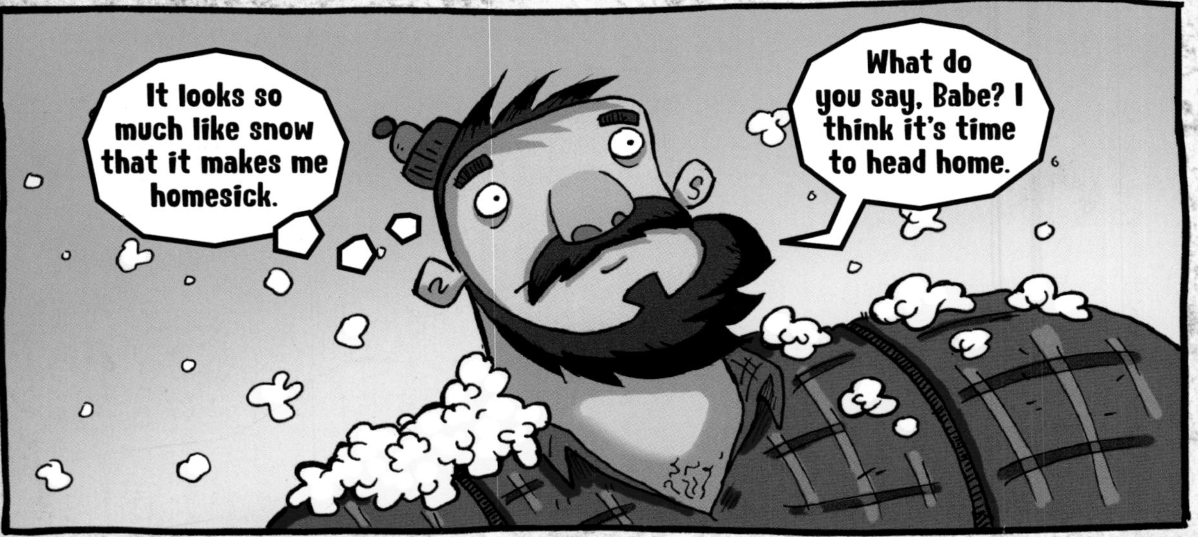
It looks so much like snow that it makes me homesick.
What do you say, Babe? I think it's time to head home.

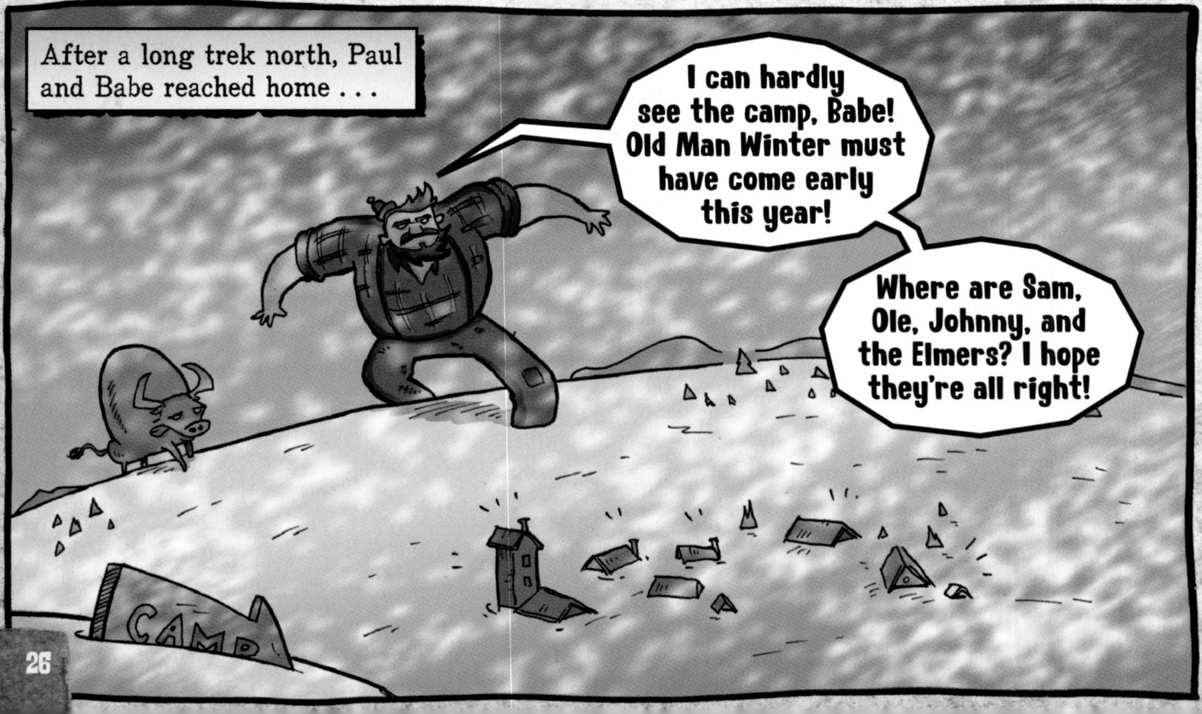
After a long trek north, Paul and Babe reached home . . .
I can hardly see the camp, Babe! Old Man Winter must have come early this year!
Where are Sam, Ole, Johnny, and the Elmers? I hope they're all right!
CAMP

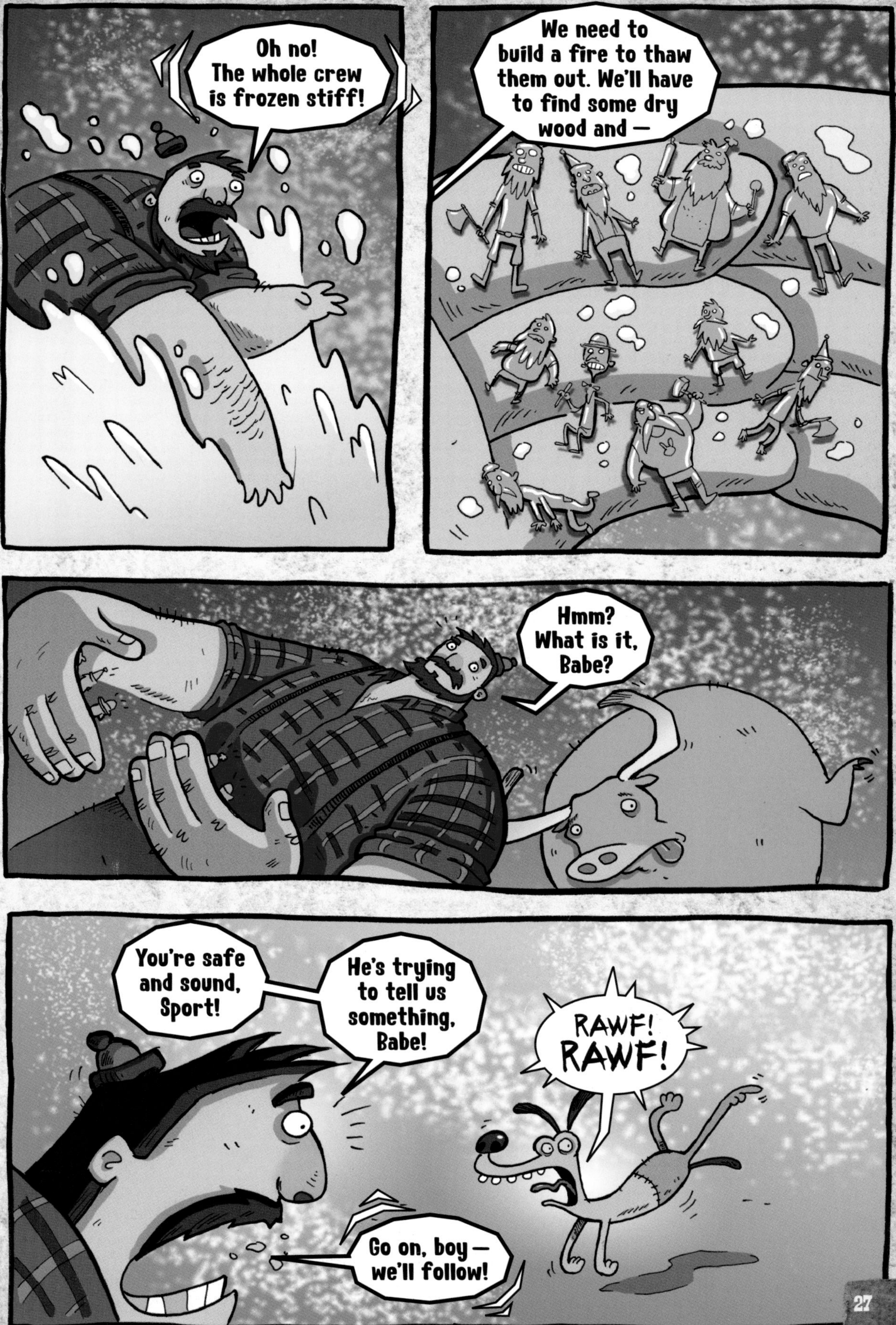
Oh no! The whole crew is frozen stiff!
We need to build a fire to thaw them out. We'll have to find some dry wood and —
Hmm? What is it, Babe?
You're safe and sound, Sport!
He's trying to tell us something, Babe!
RAWF! RAWF!
Go on, boy — we'll follow!

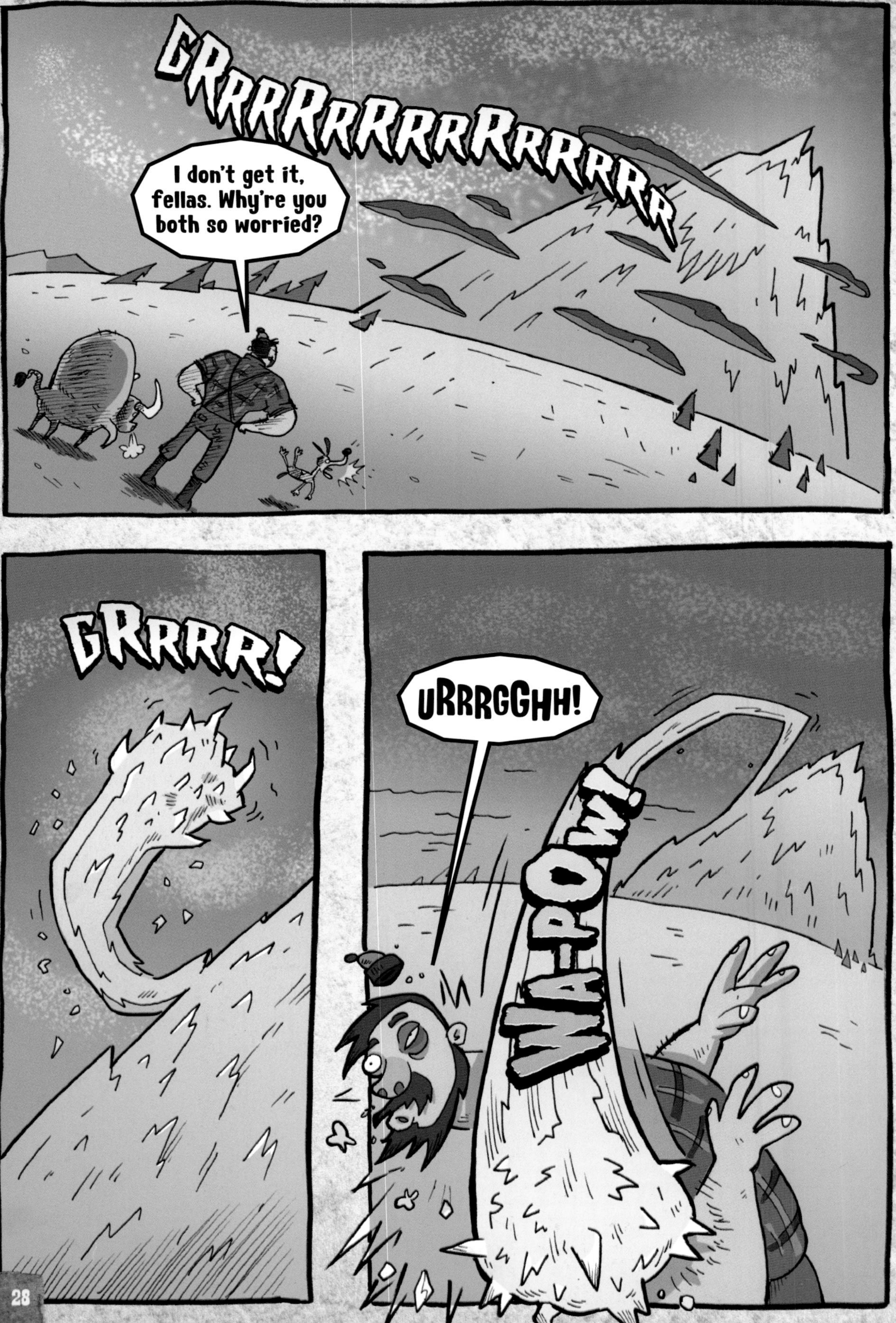
GRRRRRRRRRRRRRRRRR
I don't get it, fellas. Why're you both so worried?
GRRRR!
URRRGGHH!
WA-POW!

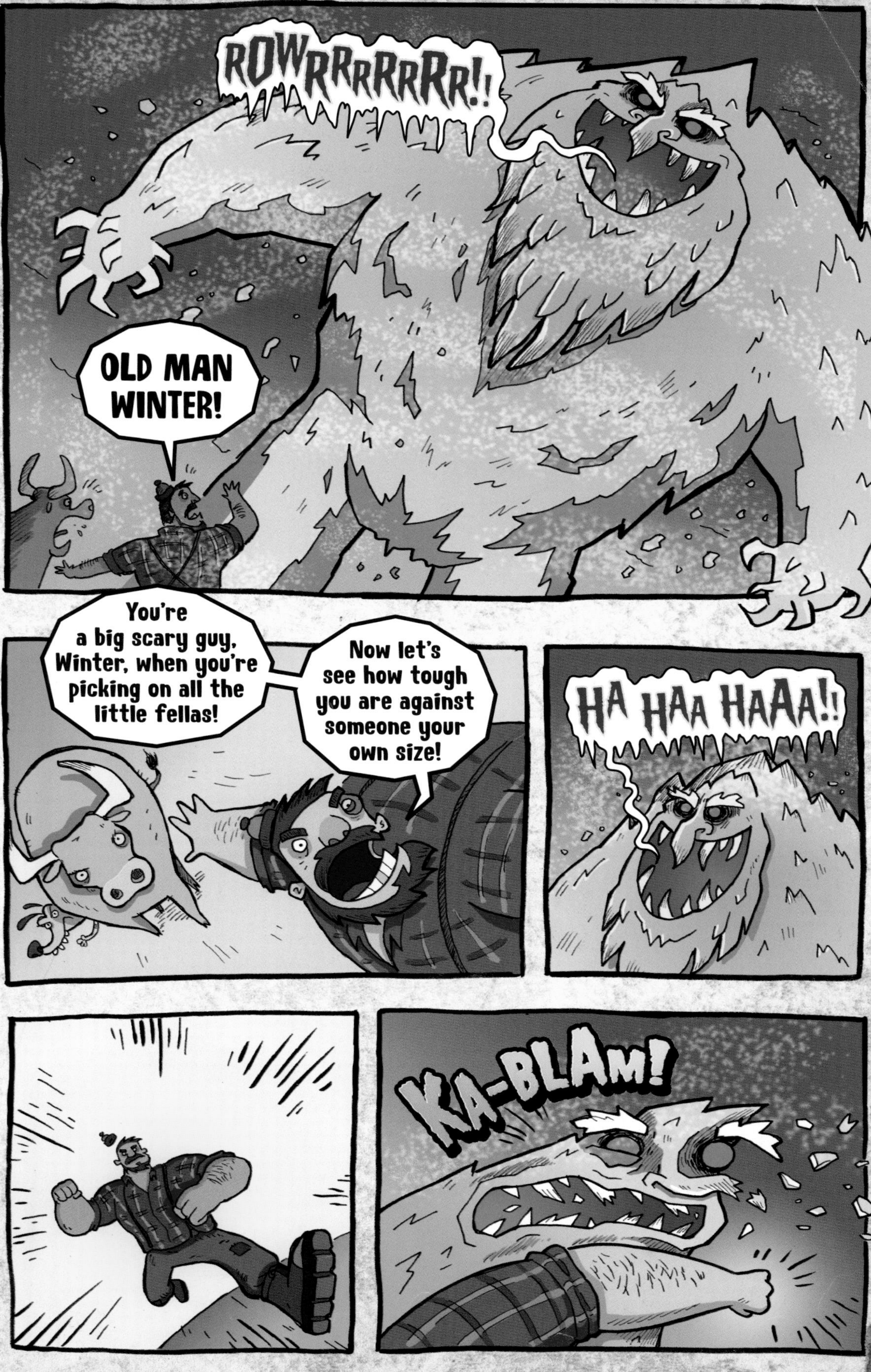

ROWRRRRRRR!!
OLD MAN WINTER!
You're a big scary guy, Winter, when you're picking on all the little fellas!
Now let's see how tough you are against someone your own size!
HA HAA HAAA!!
KA-BLAM!

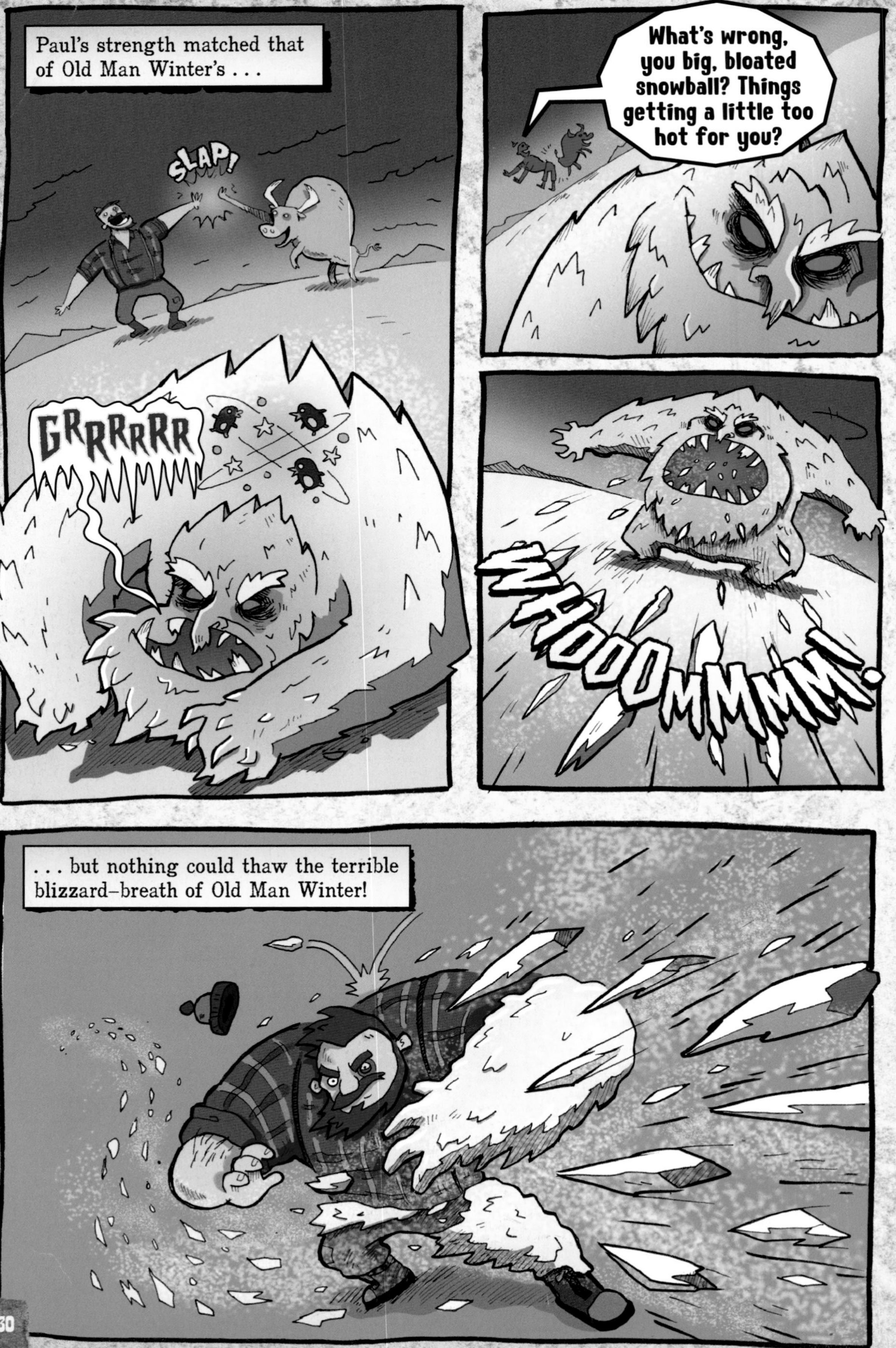

Paul's strength matched that of Old Man Winter's . . .
SLAP!
GRRRRRR
What's wrong, you big, bloated snowball? Things getting a little too hot for you?
WHOOOMMMM!
. . . but nothing could thaw the terrible blizzard-breath of Old Man Winter!

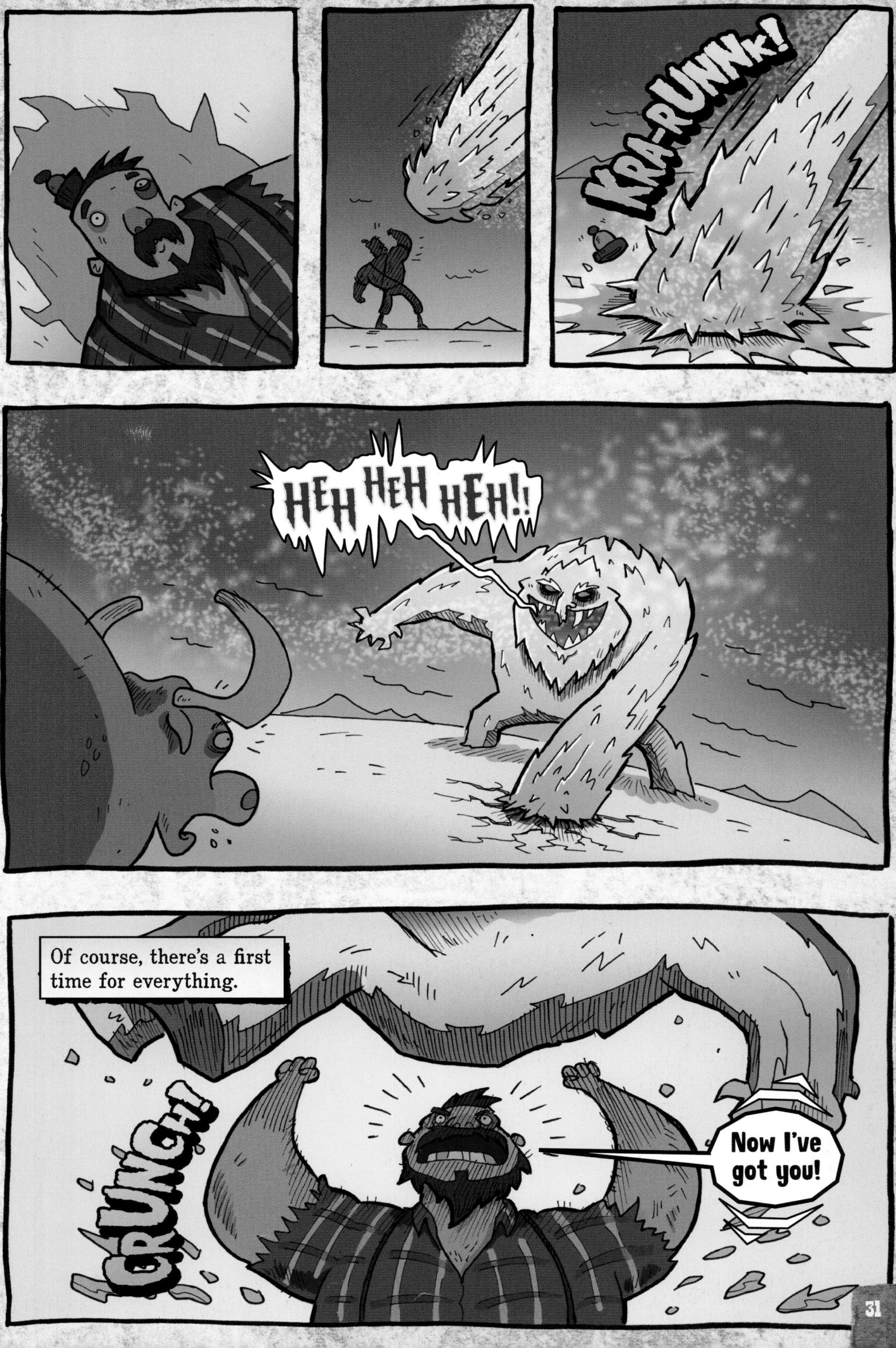

KRA-RUNNK!
HEH HEH HEH!!
Of course, there's a first time for everything.
GRUNCH!
Now I've got you!

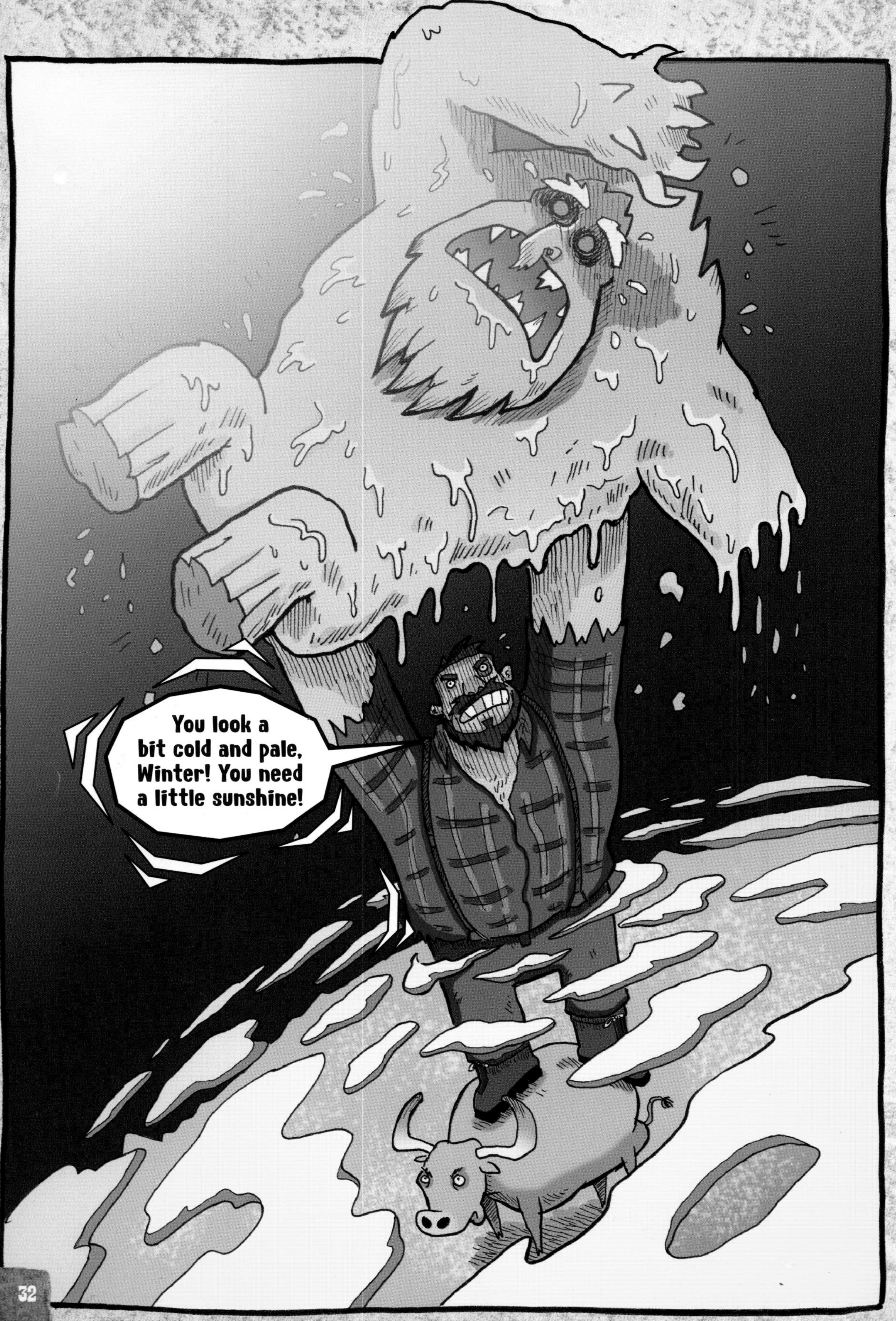
You look a bit cold and pale, Winter! You need a little sunshine!

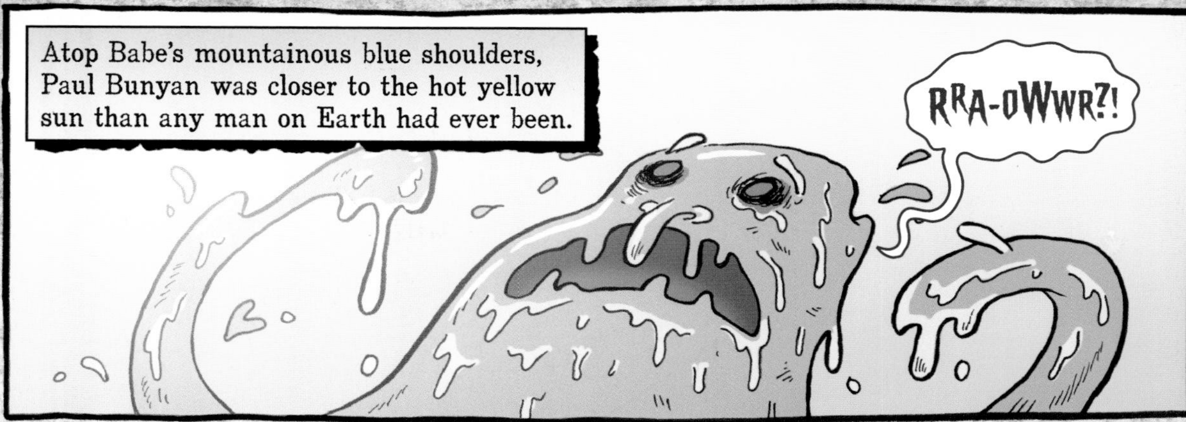
Atop Babe's mountainous blue shoulders, Paul Bunyan was closer to the hot yellow sun than any man on Earth had ever been.
RRA-OWWR?!

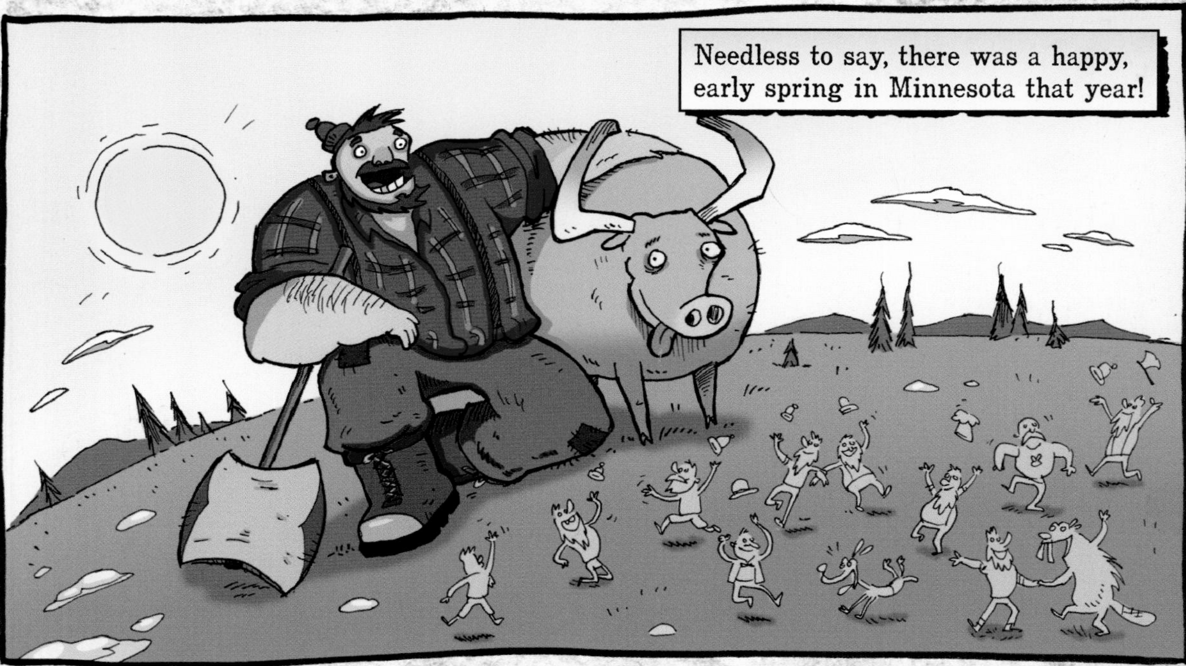
Needless to say, there was a happy, early spring in Minnesota that year!

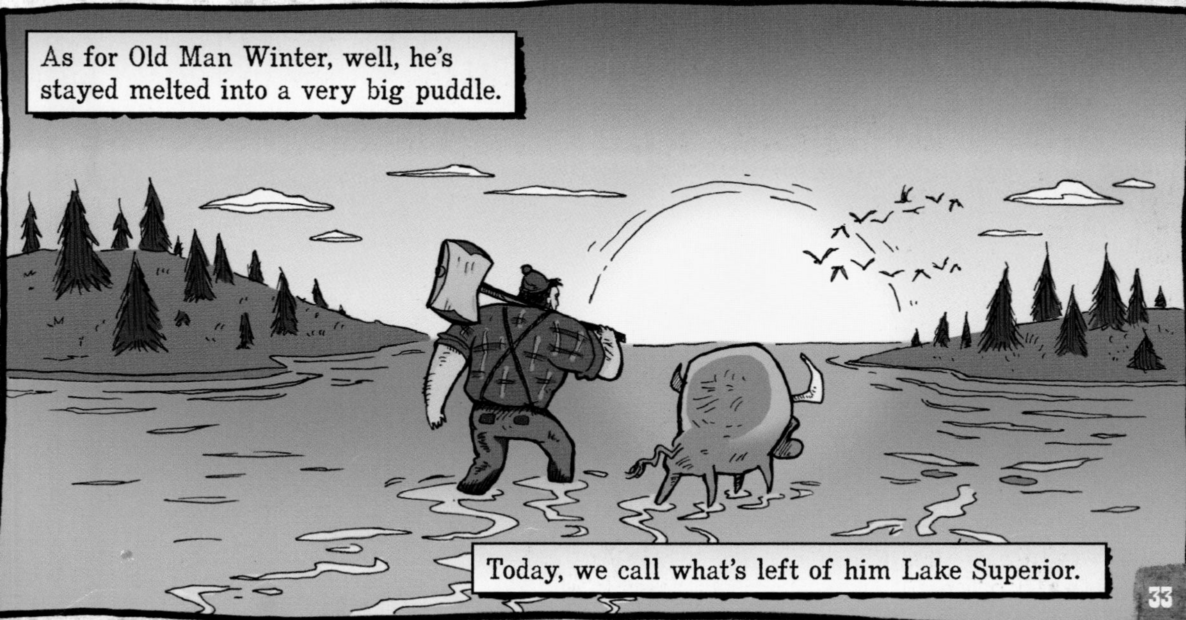
As for Old Man Winter, well, he's stayed melted into a very big puddle.
Today, we call what's left of him Lake Superior.

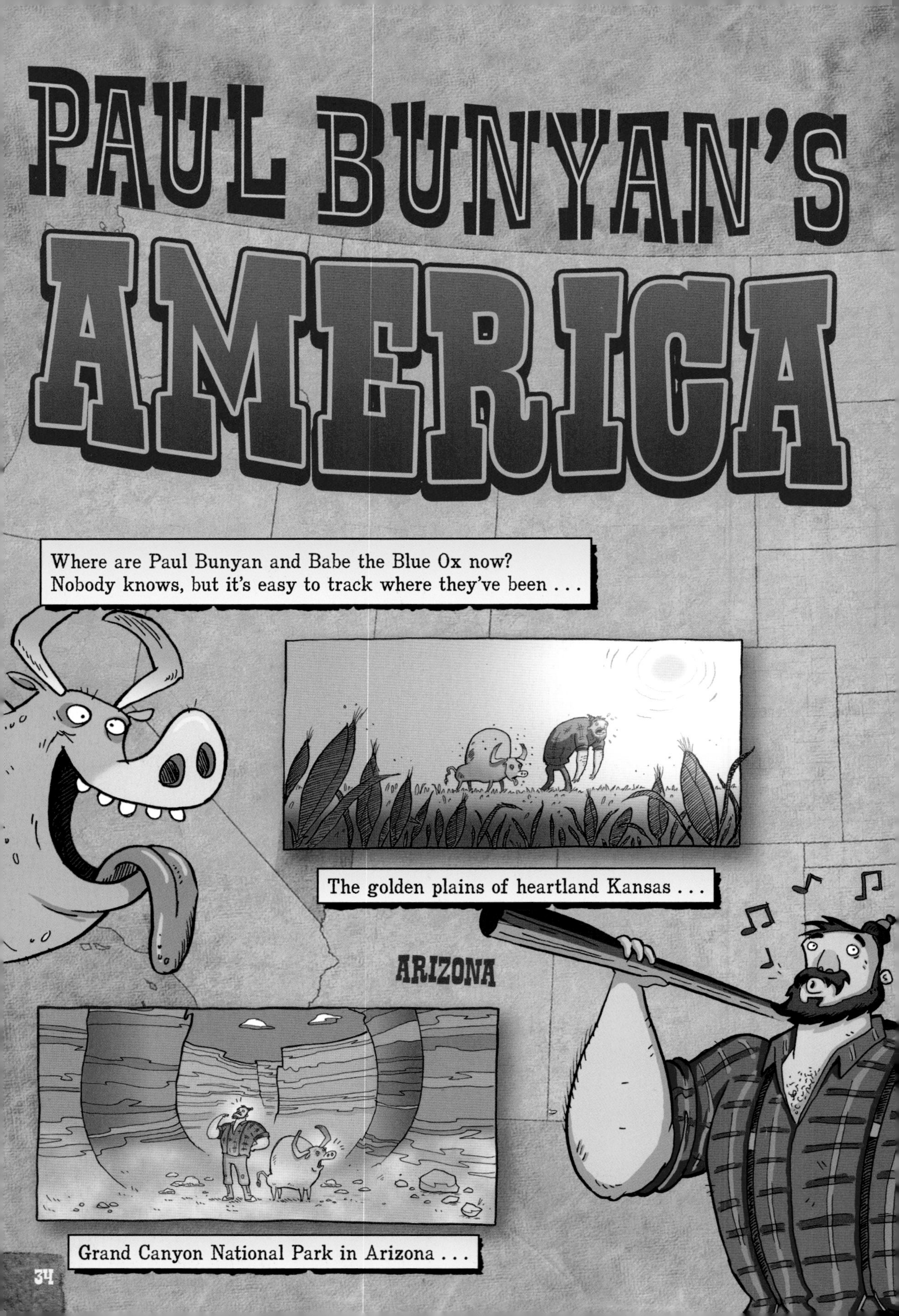
PAUL BUNYAN'S
AMERICA
Where are Paul Bunyan and Babe the Blue Ox now? Nobody knows, but it's easy to track where they've been . . .
The golden plains of heartland Kansas . . .
ARIZONA
Grand Canyon National Park in Arizona . . .

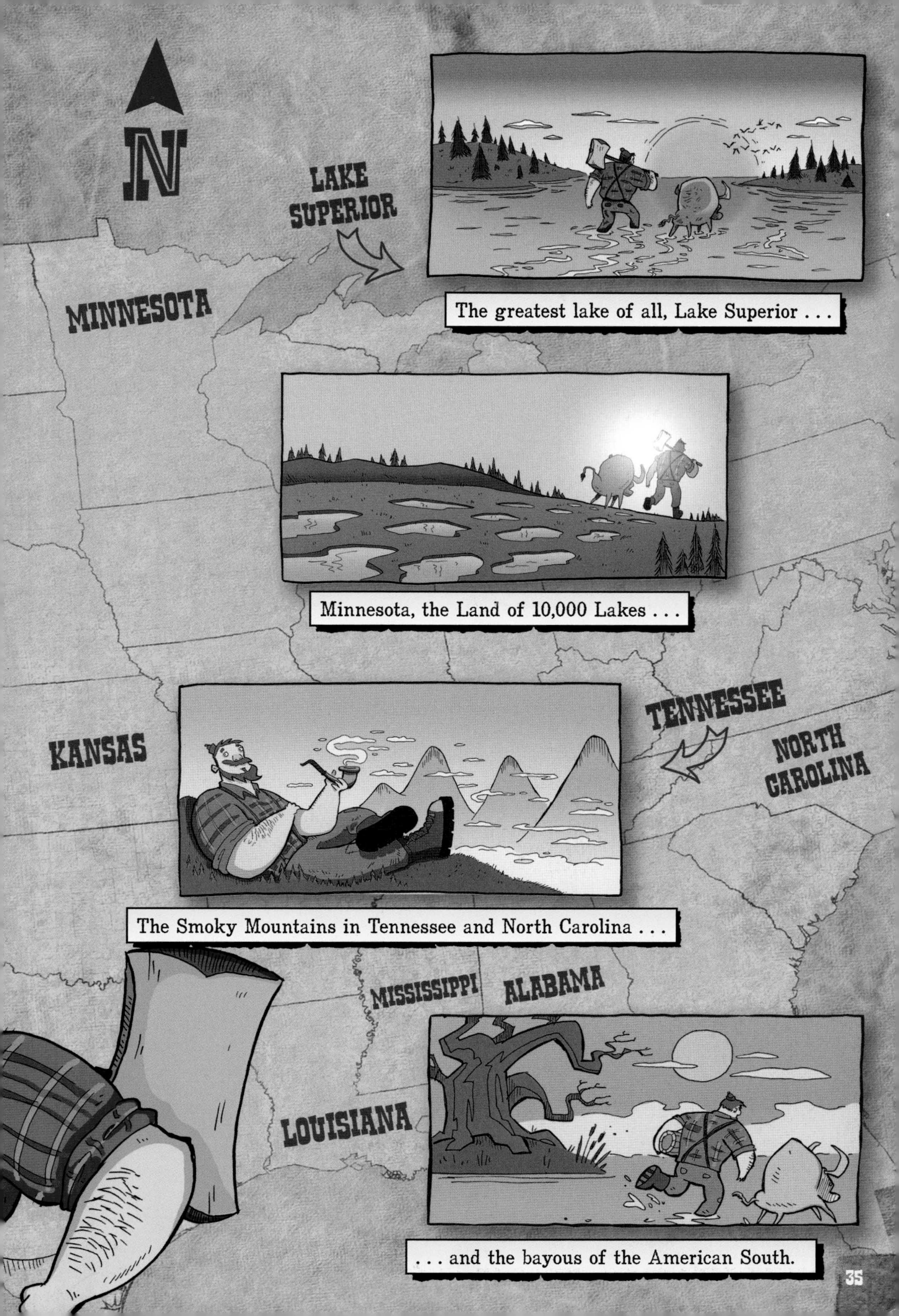

N
LAKE SUPERIOR
MINNESOTA
The greatest lake of all, Lake Superior . . .
Minnesota, the Land of 10,000 Lakes . . .
KANSAS
TENNESSEE
NORTH CAROLINA
The Smoky Mountains in Tennessee and North Carolina . . .
MISSISSIPPI
ALABAMA
LOUISIANA
. . . and the bayous of the American South.

THE END

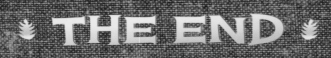

MEET THE BOOK'S CREATORS

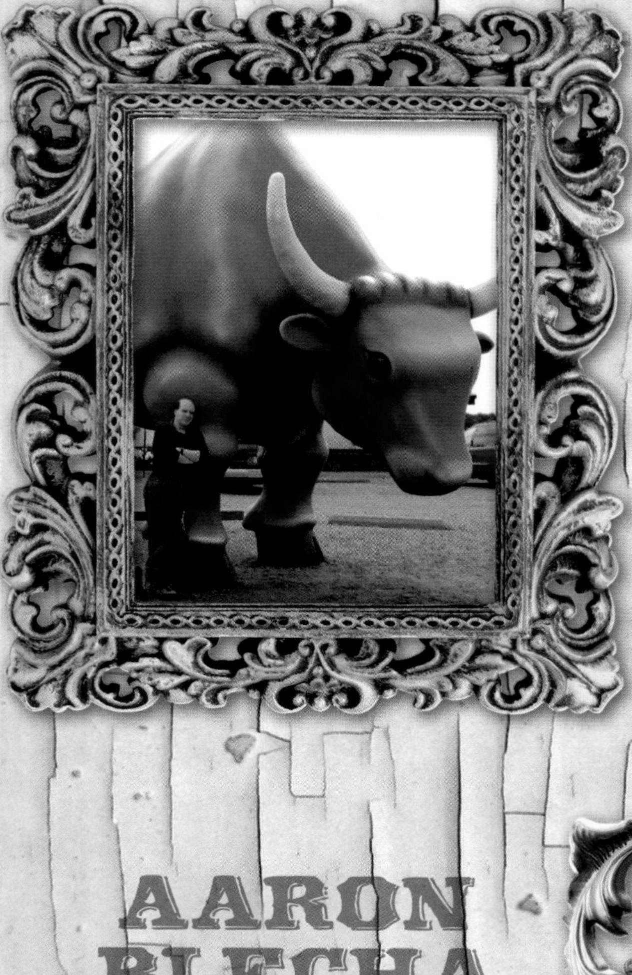

MARTIN POWELL

AUTHOR

Since 1986, Martin Powell has been a freelance writer. He has written hundreds of stories, many of which have been published by Disney, Marvel, Tekno Comix, Moonstone Books, and others. In 1989, Powell received an Eisner Award nomination for his graphic novel *Scarlet in Gaslight.* This award is one of the highest comic book honors.

AARON BLECHA

ILLUSTRATOR

Aaron Blecha was raised by a school of slimy, yet gooey, giant squids in Wisconsin. Since then, Blecha has been working for more than ten years as an illustrator and designer for a hodgepodge of fun clients in the animation, publishing, toy, and entertainment industries. After many years in San Francisco, he now calls London his home.

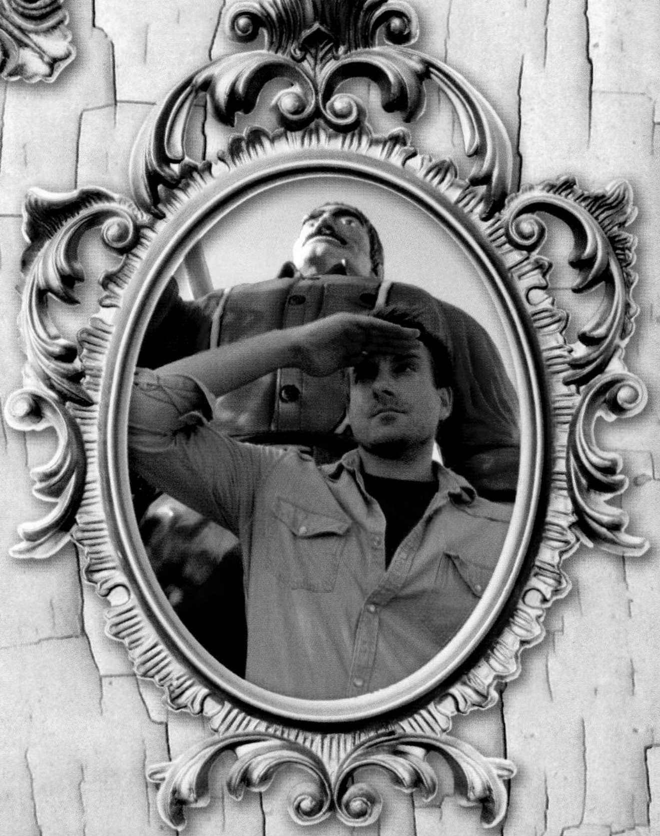

LEARN

100 PERCENT CERTIFIED GLOSSARY

attentive (uh-TEN-tiv)—if you are attentive, you are alert and paying close attention to someone or something

bales (BALEZ)—large bundles of things, such as straw or hay, that are tied tightly together

bayou (BYE-oo)—a stream that runs slowly through a swamp and leads to or from a lake or river

bloated (BLOH-tid)—swollen, often as a result of eating or drinking too much

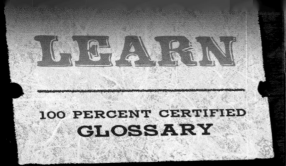

bundle (BUHN-duhl)—something wrapped up or tied together

clerk (KLURK)—someone who keeps records

molasses (muh-LASS-iz)—a sweet, thick, sticky syrup that is made when sugarcane is processed into sugar

pale (PAYL)—having a light skin color, often because of illness or fright

reversible (ree-VURSS-uh-buhl)—able to be turned around, upside down, or inside out

skillet (SKIL-it)—a large frying pan

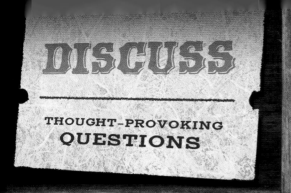

DISCUSS

THOUGHT-PROVOKING QUESTIONS

1. Many famous sites appear in this book, including the Grand Canyon and Lake Superior. Have you ever visited these places? What are some sites you've seen?

2. The tall tale of Paul Bunyan has a lot of exaggeration in it. But are there parts in this story that could be real? Explain.

3. Which of the illustrations in this book was your favorite? Why?

LEARNING IS FUN!

WRITE

ENCOURAGING PROMPTS

1. This book has all kinds of strange creatures in it, like Sport the Reversible Dog, Babe the Blue Ox, and the saber-toothed beavers. Think up your own weird creature. What does it look like? What does it eat? Draw a picture of your crazy creation.

2. Paul decides it's time to leave his parents' home and find his own path in life. Where do you think you'll be in ten years? Will you be in college? What do you want to do for a living? Write about your future.

3. Tall tales are made-up stories about how amazing things were created. Paul Bunyan, for example, created the Grand Canyon when he was wrestling with Babe the Blue Ox. Think of something amazing, and write an explanation about how it was created.

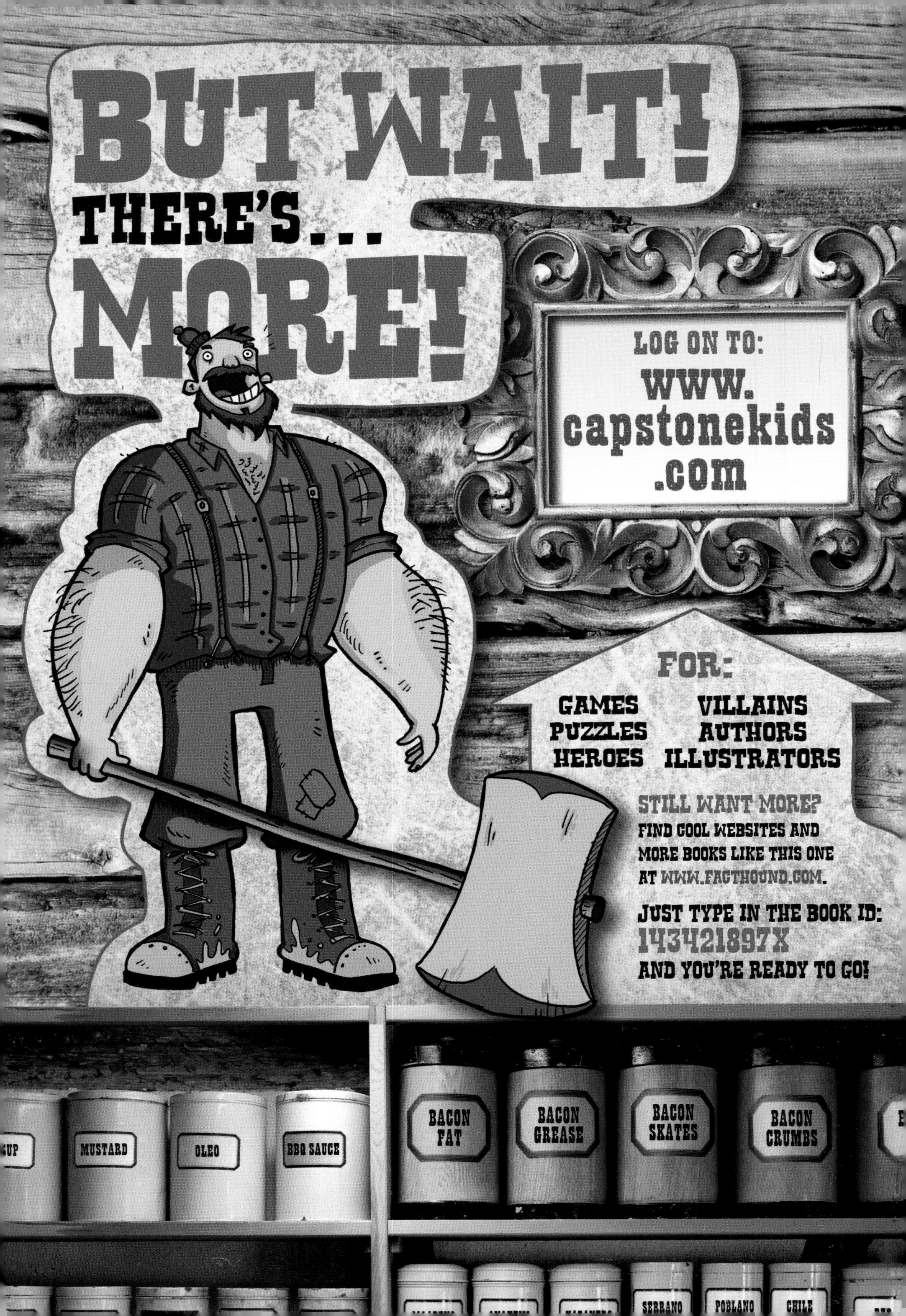
BUT WAIT! THERE'S... MORE!
LOG ON TO:
www.capstonekids.com
FOR:
GAMES
PUZZLES
HEROES
VILLAINS
AUTHORS
ILLUSTRATORS
STILL WANT MORE?
FIND COOL WEBSITES AND MORE BOOKS LIKE THIS ONE AT WWW.FACTHOUND.COM.
JUST TYPE IN THE BOOK ID:
143421897X
AND YOU'RE READY TO GO!
MUSTARD
OLEO
BBQ SAUCE
BACON FAT
BACON GREASE
BACON SKATES
BACON CRUMBS
SERRANO
POBLANO
CHILE